# PALM BEACH
# DEADLY

## TOM TURNER

D1502701

# ACKNOWLEDGMENTS

As always, thanks to Serena and Georgie for letting me badger you incessantly, 'does this character work?' 'Which of these titles do you like the best?' 'Did you understand that allusion at the bottom of page 314?' Et cetera, et cetera.

Also, thanks to new loyal readers Sheila Stallings, Lisbeth Thom, Donna Phillips, Edie Murphy and Don Scarpa. And even newer... welcome aboard and thank you, Annette Stone.

And, my old friend—who I've never actually met in person— editor extraordinaire, Ed Stackler.

# ONE

Roughly two hundred people were assembled at the 35-million-dollar oceanfront mansion of Knight Mulcahy–yes, *the* Knight Mulcahy–to celebrate his being clean and sober for three long months. The vast majority of attendees, however, were celebrating with hi-powered cocktails—shaken, stirred, and otherwise mixed—by bartenders who didn't hold back on the pour. The fact was, only about 20% of those present were actual teetotalers and many of them were being sorely tested by the sight of unrepressed inebriants whooping it up and clearly having a hell of a lot more fun than they were.

Mulcahy stood at the alcohol-free bar, a tall goblet of freshly squeezed grapefruit juice in hand, doing what he did best: Bloviate. In fact, *the Bloviator* was one of several nicknames the press had dubbed him. Another was the *Billion-Dollar Gasbag*, which was an overstatement of his net worth, but not by much.

Manning the alcohol-free bar was a white-jacketed man with spiky, platinum hair. Behind him were four shelves, all featuring bottles of water. Very, very expensive bottles of water…there to slake the thirst of Mulcahy and his fellow twenty per centers. On the top shelf was the exotic Kona Nigari at $419 a bottle, next to the more reasonably-priced Fillico (a mere $219), both products of Japan. On the shelf below was one called Bling, which had a champagne-style cork and stood tall and proud next to Veen, a product of Finland. Below them were two from Canada–One Thousand B.C and AcquaDeco—which bookended a long, svelte bottle of Tasmanian Rain, from the small island down under the Down Under continent. Below them came the more mundane Perrier, Pellegrino and other familiar brands.

For those teetotalers who wanted more than exorbitantly priced water, the bartender was whipping up non-alcoholic concoctions with flamboyant names like Fuzzless Navel (peach nectar and OJ) and Innocent Passion (passion fruit syrup, cranberry and lemon juice) and its apparent nemesis, the Evil Princess (grenadine, apple juice and a dash of vanilla syrup.)

Knight Mulcahy peered out over a cluster of his guests and saw his son, Paul, walking across the room with his arm around the shoulder of a woman Knight had never seen before. She was wearing a black silk dress designed to display maximum cleavage. She had beautiful, azure blue eyes, high cheekbones and a confident walk.

Paul had done his job better than usual.

As Knight watched his son chat up the top-heavy beauty, Ned Durrell wandered into his periphery. Ned took a four-dollar sip from his Kona Nigari and sidled up to Knight.

Knight acknowledged him with a curt nod. "Hey, Ned, what's happening, bro?"

Knight—at sixty-one—was way too old for 'bro' and the soul knob that sprouted out below his lower lip.

Durrell gave him a withering frown. "Been meaning to take you out behind the woodshed, Knight, bitch-slap you around a little."

"The hell you talking about?" Knight asked, clearly not alarmed by the threat.

"That comment on your show about *Night Wolf*," said Durrell.

Durrell was a thriller writer who'd had a modest bestseller eleven years before but not much since. *Night Wolf* was his latest, a "*USA Today* bestseller," which lacked the clout of being a "*New York Times* bestseller," but was still nothing to be sneezed at. A thumbs-up from Knight on his number-one rated radio talk show could have meant the sale of thousands of copies, but Knight had panned it. Called it a "sleeper... as in snore," among other snarky put-downs.

"What can I tell you?" Knight said. "I knew who did it on page nine. And that sex scene—" he shook his head and frowned– "I mean did you really use the phrase, 'quivering pudenda?' I guess your editor must've fallen asleep by then, huh?"

No sugar-coater was Knight Mulcahy.

"For the record, it was not 'quivering,'" said Durrell, "it was 'trembling.'"

Mulcahy, in mid-sip of his Fuzzless Navel, burst out laughing and sprayed peach nectar all over Durrell's chin. "What-the-fuck-ever," Mulcahy said. "It was 'pudenda' that was so lame. I mean, shit, man, how 'bout just calling it 'pussy' or 'snatch' or 'cooter,' something the common man can relate to."

Durrell dabbed his chin with a cocktail napkin. "Cooter, huh? Is that what they call it up in East Jesus, West Virginia or whatever the hell you come from?"

"Kentucky, my friend," Mulcahy said. "And I'd say we've beaten this subject to death, but one last thing--" Knight always got the last word-- "Any sentence with the word pudenda in it should be outlawed. Period. End of story. Sounds so goddamn biological. If you're gonna write about sex, use words that give guys hard-ons, get women stirring in their loins. Know what I mean, bro? Christ, if you can't write a good sex scene...."

Knight shook his head and walked away, leaving Durrell to finish the sentence.

Knight Mulcahy's 66-million-dollar-a-year salary gave him the right, he figured, to say any damn thing he pleased. And, the reality was, that's exactly what had made him famous. His irreverent candor. As host of a three-hour daily show focusing on politics and current events, he had 35 million listeners a week, who–if Knight told them to dive off a cliff—would do so in a heartbeat. But Knight was content just to tell them how to think, who to vote for, and what products to buy.

Another thing about Knight, as is often the case with men who have vast power, money, and ego: he was an inveterate skirt-chaser and assumed every woman on the planet found him devastatingly sexy, utterly irresistible. Even though the man was bald, eighty pounds overweight, and had the eyes of a newborn warthog.

After shoving off from Ned Durrell, Knight headed in the direction of who he hoped would be his next conquest. Olivia Griswold was the rare female who'd never had a drop of alcohol in her life, but was well schooled in other vices. Among them: cocaine and ménage a trois (viewed by many a Palm Beacher as not a vice at all, just good, clean fun with one extra participant.) Olivia was tall, red-haired and flat-out gorgeous. She worked at Preview Properties and sold high-end houses.

Knight snuck up behind her and put his beefy mitt on her shoulder.

"How ya doin', honey?" he said and, as she turned, kissed her on the lips.

"Just fine, Knight, lovely party," Olivia said, taking a step back.

Knight looked across the capacious living room and saw his wife, Jacqui, deep into it with a woman who never talked about anything except her unabiding commitment to the born-again movement.

"How 'bout taking a walk outside with me," Knight said. "It's kinda stuffy in here."

Stuffy was the last thing it was, but Olivia might have been hoping he'd tell her about a rich friend of his who was moving to Palm Beach and needed a good realtor. Or in her case, a fair to middling one.

They walked out the French doors to the back lawn, which was the size of three football fields laid side by side. It tapered down to the beach, the black ocean off in the distance. In between was an oversized infinity-edged swimming pool that had cost Knight more than half a million dollars.

No more than twenty steps outside the French doors, Knight turned to Olivia and asked, "Wanna fuck?"

Olivia was probably no stranger to being propositioned but, chances were, never this fast and with absolutely no foreplay. She laughed, shook her head and shot him a look that said, 'you naughty boy you.'

"What a romantic," she said instead. "I'm terribly flattered, but no. Just out of curiosity, where did you intend this little love-making session to take place? Roll around on the lawn or something?"

He pointed at the pool house.

"Still, no," she said.

"Okay," Knight said. "Let's go back inside."

"To that stuffy room, you mean?"

Her irony was lost on him because Knight had already moved on, wondering who to go after next. He was—quite clearly— a direct man and of the school that if you asked enough times, someone would eventually say yes. It had worked for a number of other rich, powerful men. Ted Kennedy for one, Nelson Rockefeller for another. Kennedy had drunkenly taken Knight aside once and explained to him that the *wanna fuck?* gambit beat the hell out of flowers, candy, and an extended courtship.

Knight and Olivia walked inside and Knight noticed that the queen of the born-agains was still bending Jacqui's ear.

"Well, nice chatting with you, Knight," Olivia said.

Again, the irony fell on deaf ears. "Yeah," Knight said distractedly, casting his eye around the room.

And there she was on the far side of the room, ready for the taking.

# Two

Charlie Crawford was watching Thursday Night Football when he got the call. It was the Giants versus the Eagles. Being a New York City boy, by way of growing up in Connecticut, he missed the Giants. No way was he ever going to change his allegiance and cozy up to some Florida team even though he had been in Palm Beach for almost two years. First of all, the Jacksonville Jaguars were almost in Georgia and the Tampa Bay Buccaneers were on the other side of the state somewhere and had a quarterback who had a really bad rep with women. Then there were the Miami Dolphins, who hadn't been worth watching since Dan Marino hung up his spikes back in 2000.

The dispatcher had just reported that a "big celebrity" had been found dead up on the North End but, when Crawford pressed, didn't know who it was. Crawford had recently read that Howard Stern–of all unlikely Palm Beachers–had bought a house up there somewhere and was hoping it wasn't him because Crawford still tuned into his show every once in a while for a chuckle or two. He was racking his brain, wondering who it could be, when his partner Mort Ott's radio clicked in.

"You on your way, Charlie?" Ott asked.

"Yeah, just crossed the bridge," Crawford said. "Where you at?"

"Almost there," Ott said. "Cross street's Caribbean."

"Know who the vic is?"

"Yeah, that fuckin' loudmouth, Knight Mulcahy."

"You're kidding."

Mulcahy had never been one of Crawford's favorites. But still, Ott could have at least a little respect for the recently departed.

"Gotta go, I'm at the house," Ott said. "At least fifteen bags here already."

A bag was local lingo for uniformed cops.

"Yeah, well, don't let 'em mess up the scene," said Crawford.

"If they haven't already," said Ott.

Crawford heard Ott's door slam and could picture him taking quick, purposeful strides to the house, ready to mow down anyone who got in his way.

Ott, a homicide guy from Cleveland, had come down six months before him. Numbnuts Norm Rutledge, the police chief, had introduced them, and Crawford remembered how warily Ott had eyed him. Crawford, similarly, was thinking, who is this roly-poly rube with the handlebar mustache and Earth shoes from the Nixon era.

Crawford at the time was a burned-out ex-Manhattan cop with a big rep but not much left in the tank. So he and Ott had hooked up and became a Mutt 'n Jeff combo, starving for a good murder, but never admitting it to each other. Somehow it had clicked and here they were again... another dead guy, famous this time.

Ten minutes later, Crawford rolled up the long driveway, which slalomed its way to a big contemporary house with four sides of glass. Crawford squeezed in between two cars, one with its light still going, and walked into the house. A bag guarded the door.

"Hey, Charlie," he said to Crawford, "Ott's down at the pool house."

"Thanks, man," Crawford said. "That where the body is?"

The man nodded, then lowered his voice. "And it ain't pretty," he said, "dude sprawled out on a couch, skivvies down 'round his ankles."

Crawford walked across the huge living room. There were two evidence techs there looking around for whatever it was they were looking for. One was down on his hands and knees and had plastic gloves on. Crawford nodded at the other one and opened the French doors that went out the back.

He looked across the wide lawn and saw the pool house all lit up. Four cops were combing the exterior with Maglites. Through the glass French doors he saw Mort Ott talking to Police Chief Norm Rutledge, which was high on Ott's list of least favorite things to do.

Crawford walked up to the pool house and went through the open door.

Ott saw him, bailed on Rutledge, and walked over.

Ott, at five eight, 230, and 95% bald, looked like a high-school science teacher or maybe a parole officer. His looks worked in his favor, though, since people tended to underestimate him. Crawford, six-two, 180, handsome without much fuss, could have been a model if models bought their clothes at Overstock.com

"Lame attempt to make it look like suicide," Ott said, shaking his head. "Perp shot him twice from ten feet, then put the piece in his hand."

Ott motioned for Crawford to follow him outside. Crawford followed as Ott ducked behind an areca palm and stopped in front of a window.

"While doing my usual professional investigation," Ott said, pointing at a footprint in the sand that had yellow tape around it, "I spotted that."

"Fresh all right," Crawford said getting down in a crouch. "Doesn't look like it's gonna be much help, though."

Ott nodded and focused on the shoeprint. "You mean 'cause it looks like it's a common size?"

"Yeah, eight or a nine," Crawford said, standing up.

"But at least we can rule out guys who wear fives or thirteens."

Crawford nodded. "So what's your theory?"

"Well, the obvious: Mulcahy was bangin' some chick and had an audience," Ott said. "Question is, was it a Peeping Tom? The chick's husband? A boyfriend? Or a guy who came down here to pop him?"

Crawford clicked off a few shots with his cell.

"I got some too," Ott said, turning to go back in. "Come and check out Mulcahy's body."

Crawford walked over to Knight Mulcahy's body on the beige sofa. Crawford guessed, he weighed around two hundred and seventy fleshy, untoned pounds. He was sprawled out on the sofa, but his shaved head dangled over the side. One cushion was saturated with blood and there was another pool on the heart of pine wood floor in front of the sofa.

"Two shots, chest and stomach?" Crawford asked Ott.

"Yeah," Ott said with a nod, then flicking his head. "Nice u-trou, huh?"

Crawford glanced down at the white boxers around Mulcahy's ankles which had red hearts sprinkled all over them.

"He and his wife were having a big party up at the house," Ott said. "Caterers and bartenders are still up in the kitchen. I told 'em to stick around."

"Who else is still here from the party?" Crawford asked.

"Just his wife and son," Ott answered. "She's up at the house somewhere. That's his son over there."

Ott flicked his head towards a short man in his early thirties wearing yellow pants, a blue blazer, and a patterned pocket square, talking to a uniform. He had a half-filled glass in his hand.

"What's his name?" Crawford asked.

"Paul. Rutledge told me people call him Pawn," Ott said. "Knight... Pawn, get it?"

Crawford nodded. "You talked to him yet?"

"No. I was just about to."

Crawford walked over to Paul Mulcahy, Ott right behind him.

As they approached, Paul turned to them.

"Mr. Mulcahy, I'm Detective Crawford, this is Detective Ott," he said. "We're sorry about your father's death."

Mulcahy nodded and squeezed off a quick smile. "Thanks." He didn't look as though he was anywhere near tears.

"Can we ask you a few questions?" Crawford asked.

"Sure," said Paul. "I was just telling Officer Swan what I knew."

Crawford nodded. "About how many people were at the party tonight, Mr. Mulcahy?"

"I'd say about two hundred." Paul said. "Maybe a little less."

"Is there a guest list, do you know?"

"I don't really know, you'd have to ask my stepmother about that."

Crawford watched a tech pick up something behind Mulcahy.

"You and your father, were you pretty close?" Crawford asked.

"Yeah, we were. Worked together, too."

"Oh, you did? What did you do?"

"I'm one of the producers of his show."

Crawford nodded. "And tonight, did you happen to notice your father leave the house?"

Paul took a sip from his amber colored drink. "I saw him go out the back door with a woman, but they came right back in."

Ott taking notes, looked up. "What's the woman's name?"

"Olivia Griswold."

"Can you spell that, please?"

Paul did.

"Let me ask you a direct question," Crawford said.

"Sure."

"Was there anyone at the party who, in your opinion, might have wanted to kill your father?"

Paul exhaled dramatically, then finished off his drink. "Let me tell you something you probably already know. My father was in the business of offending people, that was his shtick, I guess you could say," Paul said, with a little heh-heh-heh laugh. "But killing him? No, I can't really think of anybody he'd offended *that* much."

Ott took a step forward. "But if you had to," he said, "if

you had to come up with a list of people who might have had a motive—whatever it may have been—who would be on it?"

Paul scratched the back of his head. "I don't know, that's a tough one. Like I said, he antagonized a lot of people, some of the stuff he said on the show—"

"We just need somewhere to start," Crawford said. "Two hundred people, that's a lot of potential suspects."

"Yeah," said Ott. "Maybe you can help us narrow it down a little."

Crawford looked at Ott then back at Mulcahy. "Sorry to be so persistent, but if you had to come up with, say, five people, who would they be?"

The dramatic exhale again. "Let me think about it a little, will you?"

"Yeah, sure," Crawford said, pulling his wallet out and taking out a card. "Just give me a call."

"Will do."

"Well, thanks. We appreciate your help," Crawford said. "Again, we're sorry about your loss. We're gonna head up to the house and talk to your stepmother."

Paul nodded at Crawford, then Ott, and did his little laugh again. "Come to think of it, that list…she'd be right up there."

THREE

They first questioned the waiters, waitresses, bartenders and cooking staff, but didn't get anything of much value from them. None of them had gone outside the house and nobody had seen Mulcahy go down to the pool house.

Crawford thanked them, said they could go home, then he and Ott went and introduced themselves to Jacqui Mulcahy.

She had fiery green eyes, blond hair and a body somewhere between buxom and zaftig. Crawford could see the tan line on her breasts, which were nestled inside a tight, black cocktail dress. They were in her bedroom, which Crawford estimated was about twice the size of his entire apartment. It had a large sitting area where they were now seated. Ott was in an upholstered wing chair and Crawford next to him in an armless club chair, facing Jacqui who was slumped down in a snow-white love seat. She had a monogramed silk handkerchief in one hand and a Pellegrino water bottle in the other.

Crawford had done the standard, 'sorry for your loss' icebreaker and Jacqui was sniffling into the handkerchief.

She was about the same age as Crawford's short-lived girlfriend, Lil Fonseca, and he guessed they might have traveled in the same social circle. Lil, thirty-seven now, had owned an upscale Palm Beach gallery and went to all the charity balls. That is, until relocating to a minimum-security jail cell up in North Carolina. But that was another story.

"One of the things I don't understand," Jacqui was saying, "is why someone didn't hear the noise from the pool house."

"You mean the gun shots?" Crawford asked.

"Yes."

"Well, it is pretty far from the main house and I'm sure it was loud inside with all the people here," Crawford said.

Jacqui nodded and sniffled again.

"Ms. Mulcahy--"

Jacqui held up her hand. "Just call me Jacqui, please."

"Jacqui," Crawford said. "We asked your stepson Paul this same question: Of all the people who came to your party, who do you think might have had a motive to kill your husband?"

She looked puzzled, then she shrugged. "Well, if they were invited to the party, presumably they were all friends of Knight's and mine."

Ott shifted in his chair and cleared his throat the way he did when he had a zinger all set to come down the pike. "Yes, but there's that old expression, 'keep your friends close and your enemies closer,'" Ott said.

"I never thought of that," Jacqui said. "I just asked Knight who he wanted to invite and his secretary emailed me a list. Some of them, to tell you the truth, I barely knew. You know, like business friends or guys he played golf with."

Ott jumped in. "Where'd he play golf?"

"At the Poinciana," she said. "He had a poker group there, too."

Crawford was surprised. He figured the Poinciana was too high-brow for any card game other than bridge. "So where did they play poker there?"

"I think in the locker room," Jacqui said. "There's a little bar there, too."

Crawford looked at his partner nodding and knew what he was thinking: That was a poker game he'd want in on. All those fat cats sitting around with big, fluffy towels around their flabby waists, ready to get taken for a few hundy.

"So of the people you knew at the party," said Crawford, "can you think of anyone who might have had a reason to kill your husband?"

Jacqui tapped her fingers on the arm of the love seat, then smiled up at Crawford.

"I can think of a few who might have wanted to call him a

dirty name, or even punch him, but nobody who'd actually want to *kill him*."

'Punch him' sounded so quaint to Crawford. Like 'bop him in the nose' or 'box his ears.' "Can you tell us who they'd be?"

"Well, there's Ainsley Buttrick," Jacqui said. "He runs a fund that Knight invested in. I think Knight made some money for a while but in the last year or so the thing kind of tanked."

Despite having been an Economics major at Dartmouth sixteen years back, Crawford's basic understanding of financial matters was a little rusty. "So what exactly happened, if you remember, to the fund?"

"Well, Knight eventually pulled all his money out of it," Jacqui said. "He said on air that if you wanted to throw your money away, the Panther Fund was as good a place as any to do it. Something like that."

"The Panther Fund was the name?" Ott asked, writing it down.

"Yes, and I think Ainsley threatened to sue him, or maybe did sue him. Eventually, Knight did kind of a retraction on the show. Said the fund had good years and bad years, like many of 'em, but just so happened all the bad years were when he had his money in it. Not much of a retraction now that I think about it."

Ott was busy taking notes.

"Thanks," Crawford said. "Who else would be on the list?"

"Ah, let's see, I'd put Sam Pratt on it."

Crawford waited for an explanation.

"Sam is another friend from the Poinciana. Knight used to play golf with him all the time, but he always told me that Sam cheated," Jacqui said. "I always figured it was just sour grapes, 'cause Sam was really good and always took Knight's money. But then, apparently, Sam got kicked out of some other club that he belonged to because he actually got caught cheating. In the club championship or something."

Jesus, thought Crawford, was this how rich guys whiled away their days?

"So what was the reason for the bad blood between Sam Pratt and your husband?"

Jacqui nodded. "One day, after Knight had a few drinks at lunch–back in his drinking days–he went on the air and told the story about Sam getting caught. Apparently what happened was, he had this little hole in the pocket of his golf pants and if he ever lost a ball–you know, hit one out of bounds or in the water–he' d roll a new ball down his leg."

Pretty neat trick, Crawford thought. "And Pratt heard your husband say this on the air?"

Jacqui nodded again. "Yeah, he heard it live. Drove straight up here, absolutely apoplectic, and in the middle of the show, said he was going to, pardon my French, 'kick the shit' out of him. Meaning Knight, of course."

"Wait," Crawford said, "is your husband's studio *here*, where the show is broadcast from?"

"Yes, in the back of the pool house. It's a pretty big studio. There's a separate entrance behind the room where he was found."

"And your stepson," Ott asked. "He's the producer of the show?"

Jacqui made one of those *psshh* sounds, akin to a skeptical chuckle. "If a producer is someone who runs down to Green's to get aspirin when Knight is hung-over. Or picks up a guest for the show at the airport, then, yes, Paul was a producer."

"Ah, with all due respect, that sounds more like a go-fer," said Ott.

Ott had an inimitable way of cutting to the chase.

"Yes, doesn't it?" Jacqui said with a wry smile.

# FOUR

Jacqui Mulcahy got seriously loquacious after a while, identifying yet another possible suspect.

His name was Chuffer Church, a man, Jacqui said, she had known for the last fifteen years. Church had started a chain of chic young women's stores while still in college and by age twenty-five had sold out to the biggest apparel maker in Hong Kong. With $50 million in the bank in the early '80s, he set out to become a polo player. But after a while he got bored with horses that wouldn't do what he commanded them to do, and set his sights on winning the America's Cup. He bought a $10 million yacht and got close to winning, but then one night—drunk at the helm—he crashed it into a seawall and was lucky to survive. A series of other unrealized, expensive pursuits followed, and by age fifty-five Chuffer Church was down to his last three million.

At that point, he decided to go back to the well and start another chain of stores that sold preppy clothes. Based on his track record, he raised enough money to open three stores: in Soho, L.A., and Boston. According to Jacqui, he had approached Knight Mulcahy two years back about becoming a backer. Knight had said he'd consider kicking in ten million dollars, which would have been enough to launch five more CC Ryder stores and give Knight a ten percent ownership of the company. It turned out, though, that the three existing CC Ryder stores were sputtering. From what Jacqui had heard anyway, the preppy look wasn't so popular in LA, and in Soho the competition was intense. The Boston shop, word was, was barely breaking even.

Then one day last fall, Knight flew up to visit his daughter at Wheaton College, in a little town outside of Boston. The two went into Boston to sightsee and decided to pay a visit to the CC Ryder on Newberry Street. Knight's daughter, Annie, totally panned the place. Said there was nothing in there she'd ever wear.

"Nothing but a cheesy J. Crew rip-off," were her exact words.

That was right before Knight and Annie went to a competitor, Vineyard Vines, just down the block and came out with two full shopping bags. The next Monday, Knight had his accountant call Church and tell him he was not going forward with the deal. Chuffer screamed and caterwauled and said he had a couple hundred thousand dollars in legal fees and start-up commitments based on Knight's saying he was in. The accountant just said he was sorry.

"Still," Crawford said, playing devil's advocate, "it's quite a leap to go from your husband reneging on a business deal with Church to wanting to kill him."

"I know, except that's exactly what he threatened to do," Jacqui said.

Ott looked up from taking notes. "Church threatened to kill your husband?"

Jacqui nodded and yawned at the same time. "It got really nasty. First, he sued Knight, then, outside of court, he confronted him and said he was going to kill him. I mean, I was there. I remember."

"You remember his exact words?"

Jacqui smiled. "As a matter-of-fact, I do."

"Could you tell us what they were?"

"He said, 'You really messed things up, you fat son-of-a-bitch cocksucker. I'm gonna kill you.' Those were his exact words... verbatim. Knight told me he didn't mind 'son-of-a-bitch' or 'cocksucker,' he'd heard those before. But he was a little sensitive about his weight."

"Seems you have a pretty good memory for insults, Jacqui," said Ott.

"Yes, well, those two were pretty memorable," Jacqui said. "Kind of hard to forget."

"If it was like that between your husband and Church," Crawford asked. "Why was he at your party?"

Jacqui shook her head. "Oh, no, he wasn't. I didn't think you were just asking about people at our party."

"No, I wasn't," Crawford said. "But what about Sam Pratt? Did he come to the party?"

"Yes, he was here. Left kind of early, I think."

"And Ainsley Buttrick?" Ott asked, looking at his notes.

"Yes, he was, too," Jacqui said with a shrug. "I guess he and Knight had patched things up."

"Thank you," Crawford said. "Anybody else?"

"Well, a friend of mine told me Knight had a pretty big argument with Ned Durrell about something," Jacqui said.

The name was vaguely familiar. "Who's he?" Crawford asked as Ott wrote the name down.

"The writer," Jacqui said.

Crawford nodded. "But you don't know what it was about?"

Jacqui shook her head. "No, sorry. I just thought of someone else. Kind of in the long-shot category, though," Jacqui said. "The man in the double-breasted blue blazer."

"Who?"

"He's this guy who always shows up uninvited at cocktail parties."

"Wait, what?" said Crawford. He glanced at Ott. Ott shrugged back.

"He's a man--I think his name is Bob--who just shows up at cocktail parties. Chats up a few people, has a couple pops, a shrimp or two, then goes on his merry way. There was this joke going around that if Bob wasn't at your party, then it probably wasn't much of a party. "

"And this man was here tonight?" Crawford asked.

Jacqui laughed. "Yes, though he didn't exactly go on his merry way."

"What do you mean?" Ott asked.

"Well, what happened was Knight went up to him when he was up at the bar and confronted him. Asked him what he was doing here, having not been invited and all. And Bob—if that is his name—didn't really answer him."

"So what happened?" Ott asked.

"So Bob took his drink and just kinda walked away from Knight," Jacqui said. "But the one thing you really don't want to do with Knight is ignore him. So Knight went charging after him, asking him again what the hell he was doing here. Meanwhile, Bob was just trying to get away from him. You would, too, the way Knight gets. All aggressive and everything. So finally Knight grabbed him by the shoulder and spun him around and said something like, 'Get the hell out of here, you low-life freeloader.'"

"And what did Bob do?"

Jacqui laughed. "What any self-respecting man would do. Threw the drink in Knight's face. Then he said, 'I didn't want it anyway. Stuff tastes like rotgut.' Which drove Knight really crazy with all we'd spent on everything."

"And what did your husband do?" Crawford asked, glancing at Ott, who was glued to her every word.

"Knight grabbed his shirt--" Jacqui said, bunching up her hand just beneath her neck—"and walked him backwards across the room all the way to the front door, then pushed him really hard. I couldn't see what happened next, but I think he may have pushed him down the front steps."

Crawford glanced at Ott again. Ott looked like someone listening attentively to an announcer describing a particularly acrobatic, game-winning football catch.

"If I was Bob," Ott said, "that might be the end of my party crashing."

"Hold on." Crawford put up a hand. "I want to make sure I got this straight. This man Bob just shows up, makes himself at home and… nobody knows who he is?"

"Pretty much," Jacqui said. "I mean he dresses nicely. The same neatly pressed double-breasted blue blazer every time, usually with a stylish pocket square. His shoes are Gucci, well, knock-offs maybe."

"How do you think he finds out about cocktails parties like yours?" Ott asked.

"My theory is he drives around until he sees a bunch of cars parked on the street. Typically on a Thursday, Friday, or Saturday night. Apparently, he's been doing it for years."

"Really?" said Ott, shaking his head.

Crawford had nothing more to ask. He and Ott thanked Jacqui Mulcahy and left.

***

As they drove down the long driveway of Knight Mulcahy's house, Ott turned to Crawford, at the wheel.

"Chuffer, huh," he said. "Don't recall ever meeting anyone by the name of Chuffer before."

"Yeah, me neither," Crawford said. "'Nother thing, I haven't been to that many cocktail parties in my life, but I've never heard of a guy showing up out of the blue and helping himself to a few pops and a couple of shrimp."

"Yeah, '*The Man in the Double-breasted Blue Blazer.*' Sounds kinda like the name of a novel. You know, like *The Girl With The Dragon Tattoo* or something."

# FIVE

Juke Jackson and Eliot Segal were sitting in a corner table of Cisco's at just past 11:30 at night. Segal was wearing Wayfarers and a flat-brimmed leather hat pulled down over his long, bleached blond hair. Jackson was wearing the same shirt he wore on the cover of his latest album, *Rock 'Til Ya Drop*, the one which had recently gone platinum. The A&R guy had come up with the title and even though Juke had thought it sounded kind of cheesy, it stuck and they went with it and now it had sold north of two million copies. Juke and Eliot were around the same age, late 40s, and both were terrified about the approaching big 5-0 and the dreaded AARP 'welcome aboard' letter they had heard so much about.

"Your fans know you play?" Eliot asked.

"Shit, no, that would be a career-killer," Jackson said and laughed. "I can see it at the supermarket check-out line: "National Enquirer Reveals: Juke Jackson is a Four Handicap!"

Eliot gave him a light fist bump.

"So how'd you come up with the idea for the club?" Juke asked.

"Well, I thought about trying to join the Poinciana, but knew there was no way in hell," Eliot said. "Can you imagine them throwing out the welcome mat for a Jew talk-show host who wears a yarmulke and campaigned for Bernie Sanders."

"I'd say you got a better chance than a singer with a sleeve of biker tats and a nipple ring," Juke said about himself.

Eliot laughed. "I don't know about that."

"The expression, 'snowball's chance in hell' comes to mind," Juke said. "In both our cases."

"Yeah, exactly," Eliot said. "So anyway, I forgot about it for a while. Played golf down at the muni at the south end in disguise. Then I heard about the Mid Island having financial problems. You know, dwindling membership, the whole deal. Had my accountant check into it. Long story short, I went after it and bought it with a few other guys."

"So you got an eighteen-hole golf course. What else?"

"Eight tennis courts, two pools--one for kids and one for us who want to get as far away from kids as possible. Then there's a nice clubhouse, a dining room, the whole schmear. That's Yiddish for everything you want in a country club and then some."

Juke nodded. "So sign me up, I'm in," he said.

Eliot smiled and reached across the table to shake his hand. "Sight unseen?"

Juke nodded. "Yeah, I've heard enough," he said. "But I'm curious, what's the Palm Beach old guard make of it?"

"Are you kidding? They hate it," said Eliot. "I mean, can you blame 'em? As Jon Bon Jovi might say, *we give country clubs a bad name.* Rich, nouveau Jews, spics, schvartzes, a Russian oligarch or two...we even got a token Muslim who they probably think's gonna wade into the deli section at Publix with an AK-47 and blow everyone away."

"I like it even more," Juke said. "What's a schvartze again?"

"Black dudes," Eliot said. "We got Oprah's business manager, the Mayor of Philly, couple other brothers who made good, even that rapper A Dollar Short, or whatever his name is."

Juke Jackson laughed. "Jeez, gets better and better."

Juke saw a group of three women in their twenties approaching from the bar. One of them thrust out her boobs and ran her tongue along her upper lip.

"Incoming trio right behind you," said Juke.

The three women broke into big hero-worshipping smiles as they approached Eliot and Juke's table.

One of them put her hand to her mouth as Eliot turned around. "Ohmigod, you, too! *Ohmigod!*"

The other two simply ogled, speechless.

"Hell-o, ladies," said Juke.

"Hi," said one, her eyes going back and forth from Juke to Eliot. "I can't tell you how big a fan I am. Of both you."

"Can we-- can we-- can we get--" one struggled to patch a sentence together.

"An autograph?" asked Eliot.

"Oh, my God, that would be so cool," said the first one. "Maybe a selfie, too."

The maître d came over.

"Ladies, I'm going to have to ask you to--"

"It's okay, " said Juke, as he autographed a coaster one had thrust at him, then he stood up and put his arm around one and smiled as she pushed her iPhone camera button.

One of them mustered up her courage. "Do you... live here... in Palm Beach?"

Juke nodded.

"Yeah," Said Eliot. "Haven't been here that long."

"Wow, not exactly a place I'd think a rock star would actually... live." She said, then not wanting to leave Eliot out. "Or the best late-night talk-show host on the planet."

"Thank you, darlin'," Eliot said. "But you'd be surprised—Rod Stewart, Jimmy Buffet, Butch Trucks, all live here."

"Wow, *really*?"

Eliot nodded, finishing up the last autograph.

"Well," said the leader, "we don't want to overstay our welcome."

But the blond apparently did. "Can we just buy you a drink maybe?"

"Ordinarily, we'd buy you one," said Juke. "But, unfortunately, we're kind of in the middle of a business discussion here."

The other one grabbed the sleeve of the blond's dress. "Come on, Lily. Well, hey thanks, it was *sooo* great meeting you guys."

"Yeah," said the blond.

"Nice to meet you, too," said Eliot.

"Bye, girls," Juke said.

The girls walked away.

"Nice ass on that blond," said Juke.

"Hey, we could get 'em back."

"Nah.... What were we talking about?"

"My club," Eliot said. "Or I should say, your new club. Glad you're coming aboard and, don't worry, people'll leave you alone. Got a good foursome for you. What's your handicap again?"

"I'm a four," Said Juke.

"Well, shit, man," said Eliot, "you could be the goddamn club champ."

# Six

Mrs. Chuffer Church, or perhaps it was his girlfriend, answered the door. She identified herself as Victoria, said she'd go get 'Chuff.'

Chuffer Church walked in behind Victoria a few moments later. He had watery blue eyes, an eight-month-pregnant woman's gut, and long grey hair that curled down around his ears. Ott had looked up his address when he got in a few minutes before Crawford that morning, the day after Knight Mulchay's murder. Then they'd waited until nine, which they deemed a decent hour to show up on his doorstep.

"Hello, Mr. Church," said Crawford, "I'm Detective Crawford, Palm Beach Police Department, this is my partner, Detective Ott."

"O-kay," Chuffer said, a little uneasily. "And what can I do for you?"

"In case you haven't heard, Knight Mulcahy was killed last night." Crawford stopped to take in Church's reaction.

"What?" said Church, in apparent shock. "What happened? How would I--"

"We need to ask you a few questions," Ott said. "Mind if we come in?"

Judging from Church's body language, he did mind, but Crawford and Ott walked past him anyway.

Reluctantly, Church pointed to his living room, where the three of them went and sat down.

"Where were you between ten and eleven last night, Mr. Church?" Crawford asked.

Church's eyes bored into Crawford's. "Are you out of your friggin' mind, you think I--"

Crawford held up a hand. "Mr. Church, we're going to be asking a lot of people that question. Please, don't be offended, just, if you would, tell us where you were."

"Right here, watching a movie. You can ask her--" Church flicked his head at Victoria, who was standing behind him.

Victoria stepped forward, nodding. "'The Danish Girl' on HBO," she said. "I didn't like it, fell asleep half way through."

"Yeah, it sucked," Chuffer volunteered.

"Mr. Church," Crawford said. "Mr. Mulcahy's wife told us you once threatened to kill him."

Victoria's head snapped back in disbelief.

Church frowned, then slowly shook his head. "Oh, Christ, that was in the heat of the moment, a long time ago," Chuffer said. "Haven't you ever done something like that? Get all worked up about something? You don't mean it, just blurt it out."

"Threaten to kill somebody—can't say as I have," Crawford said, though he remembered saying he was going to kick someone's ass into the end of next week a few times.

"So that was it?" Ott said. "Just a threat, with no intention of carrying through with it?"

"Yeah, that's exactly what it was."

"So you never left here last night?" Crawford asked.

"No," said Church.

Crawford glanced over at Ott. He didn't have anything more. Crawford got to his feet.

"Okay, well, thank you, Mr. Church," then nodding to Victoria, "You, too, Mrs. Church."

"It's Smith," she said.

"Thank you, Ms. Smith," Crawford said, turning, walking out the door and down the steps, Ott right behind him.

Crawford turned to Ott. "Guy may have lost a couple hundred thou on that Mulcahy deal that blew up," he said as they walked past a gleaming green Aston Martin, "but he's clearly a long way from food stamps."

\*\*\*

Next stop was Sam Pratt, the man with the alleged hole in his golf pants. Crawford had called him on the way over to Chuffer Church's house and set up an appointment at ten. Pratt lived on Golfview Road, a chip shot from the Poinciana club.

He answered the door in green golf shorts and a baby blue golf shirt that had a tiny chipmunk on the breast pocket. Crawford assumed that must be the logo of a fancy club somewhere.

They introduced themselves and Pratt invited them to come inside. They walked through a lavishly decorated living room out onto a loggia overlooking a pool. A naked woman was doing laps in the pool.

"Don't mind her," Pratt said. "She's like this physical fitness freak, does a couple hundred laps a day."

Judging from his long look, Ott didn't mind her at all.

"So ask away, and contrary to what you may have heard, I am *not* happy that Knight Mulcahy was killed," Pratt said.

When Crawford had spoken to Pratt on the phone, he'd told him he wanted to ask some questions about his relationship with Mulcahy. Pratt responded matter-of-factly, and without apparent grief, that he had gotten word Mulcahy had been killed. He'd also added, quite forthrightly, that they'd had their differences and weren't really friends anymore, but Pratt was still sorry he was dead.

"Mr. Pratt," Crawford started out, "Knight Mulcahy's wife, Jacqui, said you threatened him after he told a story about you during his radio show. Is that--"

"Absolutely true," said Pratt. "What that bastard did was inexcusable. You don't go around maligning a purported friend of yours, based on some bullshit locker room rumor."

"So it wasn't true?"

"'Course it wasn't true," Pratt said. "Here's the long and the short: those goddamn Poinciana locker-room gossipmongers were the source of a bunch of Knight's half-assed stories. His Bloody lunches were where they came from."

Crawford moved closer to Pratt.

"Bloody lunches?"

"Yeah, see what happened was Knight would play eighteen first thing in the morning, before his show. Then he'd hang out in the locker room for a while, shootin' the shit, hearing whatever cocked-up rumor was making the rounds. Then he'd have lunch. His lunches were notorious—a chopped salad and three big, ol' Bloody Mary's–this is before he quit the booze a month ago or whenever. Then he'd drive up to his house—weave up is more like it—go into his studio, and do his show. Half the time at least semi-shitfaced."

Crawford glanced over at Ott, who had shot a look over at the nude swimmer. Ott turned--caught in the act--a guilty look on his face.

"So they let him go and do his show like that?" Ott asked, to let Crawford know he was paying attention, "*Semi-shitfaced?*"

"Who's they?" said Pratt. "Not like there was someone with a breathalyzer up there. Only two people were his retard son and his sidekick, Skagg Magwood."

"Skagg Magwood? Never heard that name before," said Crawford. "Who's he?"

"He's Knight's redneck buddy from Alabama or wherever the hell they came from. The two grew up together. Skagg was—I can't believe I'm saying *was*—Knight's one-man posse."

"How you spell his name?" Ott asked.

"S-k-a-g-g M-a-g-w-o-o-d," Pratt said. "Pretty sure there are two G's anyway. He's the guy on the show who Knight refers to as 'Cousin.' You know…the guy who never speaks, but who Knight talks to in those asides of his."

"I'll take your word for it," Ott said. "Never listened to the show."

"I know who you mean," Crawford said, nodding.

"You might want to talk to him," Pratt said. "Word was Knight paid him McDonald's wages even though Skagg felt he was a big part of the show--" Pratt laughed. "Even though all he did was sit there. Same goes for the retard son. Got paid peanuts, too."

Crawford was glad to get a new suspect, though aware Pratt might be trying to take the spotlight off himself. "So did you happen to notice anything unusual last night at Mulcahy's party?"

"I don't know what you mean by unusual. It was the standard Palm Beach circus. I didn't even talk to Knight," Said Pratt. "Gave him a nod from across the room. That was about as close as I got."

"Never went down to his pool house then?" asked Ott.

"Never left the house, until Laurie--" Pratt flicked his head in the direction of the swimmer-- "dragged me out of there. Told me she had had about enough Knight trying to grope her."

Out of the corner of his eye, Crawford saw Laurie walk up the steps in the shallow end of the pool, completely naked, then towel off.

Pratt looked over at her and seemed to chuckle to himself. Like his wife parading around in the nude was just part of the Palm Beach circus.

\*\*\*

Ten minutes later, Crawford and Ott walked out of Sam Pratt's house to their car.

"He Canadian or something?" Ott asked, opening his car door.

"Oh, you mean when he said his wife had 'a-boat' enough of Mulcahy trying to grope her?"

"Yeah, said it another time, too," Ott said, sliding into his seat.

"I don't know maybe," Crawford said, snapping his seat belt. "He our killer?"

"I think, based on what we got so far, he goes down as an 'unlikely.' What do you think?"

"I agree," said Crawford.

"I also think," Ott said, "speaking of killer, ol' Laurie's got herself a killer body."

Crawford shook his head and chuckled. "As usual, Mort, your

powers of observation are next to none."

# SEVEN

It turned out that Skagg Magwood lived exactly a block away from Crawford's place in West Palm Beach. Which is to say, a middle-class neighborhood two miles away from Palm Beach, but similar to the socio-economic distance between Manhattan and the Bronx.

If you didn't know any better, you'd think Skagg Magwood was a redneck hillbilly. He had a beat-up trailer in his back yard and answered the door wearing a cowboy hat and a work shirt with fake pearl snap buttons.

"Yassir," he said, looking out at Crawford and Ott from his front door.

"Mr. Magwood?" Crawford said, squinting up at him. "Skagg Magwood?" Crawford liked saying the name. It had a certain ring.

"Yassir, that would be me."

"I'm Detective Crawford--" he gestured toward his partner, "this is Detective Ott."

"Ott," said Magwood, glancing up at Ott, "that's a kinda peculiar name. Scandinavian?"

"German actually," Ott said.

"I think there's an alt band by the name of Ott." Magwood said.

"I wouldn't know," Ott said. "Mr. Magwood, you've heard that Knight Mulcahy was killed last night, right?"

Magwood nodded. "I was just going over to Palm Beach to pay my respects to his wife."

Crawford nodded. "According to what we've heard, you knew him about as well as anyone."

"Well, I knew him longer than anyone. Plus, of course, I worked for him."

Crawford nodded. "For how long?"

Magwood scratched the three-day growth on his chin. "Somewhere in the neighborhood of thirty years. Back in Louisville, a little 500 watt station, I did the grunt work and he did the talking."

Sounded like that was still the case until yesterday, Crawford thought. "So when Mulcahy and you prepared for his shows, what exactly was involved in that?"

Magwood looked blank.

"I mean, Mulcahy didn't just get on the air and wing it or did he?" Crawford asked.

"Well, actually he kinda did, but not always," Magwood said, shifting from one leg to the other.

"How do you mean?" Ott asked.

"Well, basically, we'd put together a list of subjects. Say like, 'Obama-ISIL' or 'Hillary-Vince Foster', then he'd pretty much wing it from there. Like talk about how Obama was the only guy in the world to call ISIS ISIL. Or how Hilary was behind Vince Foster's suicide."

"So what about when he got talking about local guys and how bad their stock fund was or them cheating at golf?"

"You mean Ainsley Buttrick and Sam Pratt?" Magwood said with a grin.

"Yeah, exactly."

"Sometimes they'd be on the list, and sometimes he'd just– outta the blue–rip 'em a new one."

"So like maybe, 'Obama-ISIL, Hilary-Vince Foster, Pratt-golf?'"

Magwood scratched his chin again. "Somethin' like that."

"And these guys—like Pratt and Buttrick—did Mulcahy ever talk to you about being scared of either one of 'em? Or think they might've wanted to kill him?"

Magwood gave his chin one more scratch. "Cause of things they said, you mean?"

"Yeah, exactly," Crawford said.

"Nah, I don't think so," Magwood said. "It was just guys getting pissed off at each other–the way they do. You know how it is. Even that guy Church who actually did threaten to pop him, I'm pretty sure Knight didn't take him too seriously."

Crawford nodded and looked over at Ott. Next batter?

Ott cocked his head. "Was there a list of subjects for next week, by any chance? People who Knight was planning to talk about next?"

"Well, Trump as usual," Magwood said. "Knight couldn't get enough of 'ol Bad Hair."

"How about local people?" Ott asked.

"I remember Juke Jackson was on the list," Magwood said. "Knight played golf with the guy, said he was like incredibly good. Hustled Knight out of a couple grand. Turned out he's a three-handicap or something. He kinda forgot to tell Knight that."

Crawford shook his head. He knew Juke Jackson had recently bought a house in Palm Beach, but a three handicap? His idol had just gone up another notch.

"Yeah," Magwood said. "Three-hundred-yard drives… guy can play."

"Really," Crawford said, admiringly.

Magwood nodded his head. "Oh, also, this guy Earl Hardin was on the list, and Sam Pratt again."

Ott wrote down 'Earl Hardin' and looked up, "Who's Earl Hardin?" he asked.

"I don't really know," Magwood said. "A guy who lives around here."

"About Pratt? What was he going to talk about this time?" Crawford asked.

Magwood shrugged. "Don't really know that either," he said. "Knight didn't fill me in, but something about a play, I think."

"A play?" Crawford asked.

"Sorry, that's all I know," Magwood said.

"So," Ott jumped in, "knowing him as well as you did, what's your theory about who might've killed him?"

"I been racking my brain since it happened," Magwood said.

"When did you first hear?" asked Ott.

"Last night. About two in the morning. His son Paul called me."

"Pretty broken up, huh?" Ott asked.

Magwood thought for a second, then cocked his head. "You'd think so, wouldn't you?" he said. "But ol' Pawn sounded kinda... relieved."

# EIGHT

Crawford was in a booth at Three Petes having lunch by himself.

The Pete with the comb-over and gimpy leg--not to be confused with the short, squatty one, or the one with the purple birthmark on his face--had just served him a bowl of clam chowder and a Caesar salad.

He was digesting his food along with everything else he had just heard related to the murder of Knight Mulcahy and was 90% sure he hadn't talked to the murderer yet.

He looked around the restaurant and took in his fellow diners. A casually-dressed, blue-haired woman in her eighties who he guessed had probably shrunk a few inches over the last ten years. Four women in halter tops and clingy sun dresses in their thirties, yakking away non-stop all at once. One had looked over at him a couple of times, winking once. A distinguished man--fifties or sixties--in a double-breasted blue blazer over a white sports shirt. *Hmmm*, Crawford thought, looking twice at the jacket. But it wasn't like he could go up and ask him if he had been to any good cocktail parties lately.

He leaned back and thought about his two years in Palm Beach. Mostly good. Sometimes bizarre. His thoughts came in a wave, Palm Beach was kind of a town that was hard to describe. Beautiful, big houses, often way-over-the-top in their grandiosity and look-at-me ostentatiousness. Incredible, lush landscapes everywhere you looked, but almost obscene when you figured what it all cost and started thinking about the homeless just across the bridge in West Palm. Not that Crawford was about to get preachy or sanctimonious.

Also--he wondered--was there a cleaner place in America than Palm Beach? You really could, as the old cliche went, eat off the streets. And pity the poor guy on the beat-up bike, who you'd see in many other towns, going around looking for cans. Trying to fill up his Hefty trash bag and get a nickel for each one. He'd be lucky to find two cans in a whole day in Palm Beach. The streets were just so damn immaculate. It was almost as if some higher authority had decreed that if you dropped a candy-bar wrapper on the side walk, you'd be put in prison for life.

His mind was a million miles away when he heard the familiar voice right behind him.

"Hey, hot shot, couldn't find anyone to break bread with?"

He smiled up at Rose Clarke and patted the banquette next to him. "Just sitting here, hoping you might happen along."

Rose was a five-foot-ten blond who prided herself on being gym-trim and tight. She was also--at least as far as Crawford's unscientific ranking system went--in the top 1% of the best-looking women in Southern Florida. And, by far and away, the best real-estate agent in Palm Beach, with annual sales of high-end properties of more than $300 million a year. Even going back to the bad old days in 2008. She had also been invaluable--a couple of times--in providing him with information about people who had factored into murder cases. If you wanted the scoop, Rose was the one to talk to.

"What's the good word, Charlie?" she asked, sliding into the booth and seeing the headline of his Palm Beach *Post*. "So the Mouth of the South is no longer with us. *Quelle domage*."

That was another thing about Rose--the girl was blunt. Particularly about people she didn't like.

"Did you know him?"

"Too well. He bought his house from me," she said. "Hondled on the price, on the commission, on the attorney's fee, you name it."

Crawford shook his head. "That's amazing. With his kind of money?"

"Some of the cheapest men I know are some of the richest."

"Guess that's how they got that way."

"Yeah, but, I mean, come on," she said. "He was just cheap

to be cheap."

"You gonna have something or just pick on those who can't defend themselves?" Crawford said. "I'm buying, by the way."

Crawford flagged down the short, squatty Pete.

He came over, pad in hand. "Just the house salad, Pete, with gorgonzola, please," she said.

"You got it, Ms. Clarke," he said and walked away.

"Sure is easy," Rose said. "Everyone who works here named Pete."

Crawford pointed at the *Post*. "Okay, out with it: your theory about who killed Mulcahy. I'm sure you spent a good part of this morning while doing your Downward Dog chewing it over."

"You know me too well," she said. "I've gotten too damn predictable."

"Yeah, and my prediction is you have a laundry list of possible suspects."

"More like half of Palm Beach," Rose said. "Paul Mulcahy wants his inheritance; Jacqui...ditto; Brewster Collett wants to marry Jacqui; Chuffer Church got screwed by him and couldn't stand him; Lila Moline was sick of him stringing her along. I mean, Christ, even the damn mayor had a motive."

"Whoa, whoa, slow down, you're going way too fast," Crawford said.

"I was just getting started," said Rose.

"Okay, first of all, who is Brewster Collett?"

"A formerly rich guy who lost his inheritance and is one of Jacqui Mulcahy's toy boys. I heard he tried to get Jacqui to divorce Knight but she told him she'd only get three million bucks if she did."

"So Mulcahy had her on a tight little pre-nup?"

"Exactly," said Rose, "but if he died, she got half."

"His son Paul gets the other half?"

"Paul and his spoiled-rotten sister."

"Gotcha," said Crawford. "Okay, so Lila Moline, who's she? Never heard that name before."

"She runs a little antique shop on South County and Worth. Les Trucs, it's called. Overpriced French junk."

"Yeah, but who is she?"

"One of Knight's girlfriends," said Rose. "The one he promised he'd divorce Jacqui and marry."

"Knight and Jacqui had the proverbial marriage-made-in-heaven, I see," Crawford said. "How'd you find this out about Lila Moline, I mean?"

"Same way I find out everything. Drink less than the people I'm with and listen really well. But in her case, she got drunk one night and told an agent I work with the whole squalid story."

Rose's salad showed up. "Thanks, Pete. Looks *di*-vine."

Pete nodded, smiled and walked away.

"You said Jacqui's 'boyfriends' and Knight's 'girlfriends'... plural."

"Yeah?"

"So are you saying--"

"I'm saying, by my last count Knight had three and she had two. But that could be low."

Crawford shook his head. "Really?"

"Really." Rose tore into her salad.

"What about this guy Jacqui Mulcahy told me about, some mook who goes around crashing cocktail parties?"

Rose laughed. "I love it when you use those colorful detective words," she said. "The *mook* you're talking about is the man in the double-breasted blue blazer."

"Yeah, exactly. What do you know about him?" Crawford asked.

"Not much," Rose said. "But I've probably seen him at at least a dozen cocktail parties. Guy gets around. Wait, you're not thinking he could be your man?"

"I don't know," Crawford said. "I'd at least like to question him. You never caught his name, did you?"

"I think it's John," Rose said. "But, sorry, absolutely no idea what his last name is."

Crawford took a slow pull on his water. "And the mayor? You mentioned her. How's she factor into this little soap opera?"

"I heard one time when Knight got a fifty dollar parking ticket he went into a long rant about how corrupt the Palm Beach local government was," Rose said. "Called her a greedy dyke or something subtle like that."

Crawford shook his head. "Jesus, the guy was a real loose cannon," he said. "But I don't think I need to put her on my interview list."

Rose nodded and put down her fork. "Yeah, probably not. Still, I can guarantee you there weren't a lot of tears shed in this town in the last couple of days."

"How about you? What was your feeling about the guy? Aside from him being a world-class hondler."

Rose laughed. "Hey, I could be a suspect, too, I guess," she said, leaning forward. "Supposedly he told a bunch of his pals in the Poinciana locker room I was a lousy real-estate broker."

"Based on what?" Crawford asked. "I mean, you sell half the houses in Palm Beach."

"How the hell do I know? Based on the fact that I didn't laugh at one of his lame jokes maybe," Rose said. "Or suck up to him so he wouldn't rip me on his show."

She took another big bite.

By the time they left Three Petes, Crawford literally had--not including the mayor or Rose herself--between four and five new suspects. Granted, some of them were long shots but they all seemed worth checking out.

*** 

Crawford walked up to Ott's cubicle at the station house and heard him on the phone.

"Thanks," Ott said. "And no DNA to speak of?"

Then Ott nodded a few times. "Okay, so let me know if you run across anything in ballistics. Yeah, I know the serial number was filed off the weapon, but maybe you'll come up with something else."

Pause. "Yeah, I know. Thanks anyway."

Ott looked up at Crawford. "Evidence techs are comin' up empty."

"Given the lack of prints from the scene, I'm not surprised."

"But I got something good," said Ott. "You know how our boy Chuffer said that movie was on from nine to eleven. He watched it, then lights out."

Crawford nodded.

"Well, I checked and it actually was on from seven to nine," Ott said. "But the best part is I got him on a security cam coming out onto North Lake Way at 10:05."

"Well, well," Crawford said, "guess we need to show up on ol' Chuffy's doorstep again."

Ott nodded. "Yeah, find out where he was headed in that sweet, little Aston-Martin."

# NINE

Algernon Poole, tall, poised and striking-looking, walked into Jacqui Mulcahy's drawing room. The room was mainly browns and dark blues and seemed appropriate colors for the room of one deep in mourning. But Jacqui was pretty much over her husband's death two nights ago and seemed to have moved on.

Jacqui stood up and gave Algernon a kiss on the lips, then threw her arms around him.

After a moment Algernon, pulled back. "Everything okay with you, my love?"

"Yeah, it's just going to be an endless parade of accountants and lawyers for a while," she said, sitting back down.

"Then what?" he asked, sitting down next to her.

"Then I thought I might go on a little cruise," she said. "There's this Cunard Northern Europe and British Isles one I've been dying to go on. Kept trying to get Knight to go but he didn't want to take a week off and have lousy weather."

"It's not always like that," Algernon said. "When would you go?"

"Just as soon as I get my gazillions," Jacqui said. "And if you're nice to me, maybe I'll have a ticket for you. You could watch your ancestral castle pass by from the Sandringham suite on the *Queen Mary 2*."

"That sounds lovely," Alergnon said, "only problem is, the 'ancestral castle' is about thirty miles inland."

"Ah, too bad," said Jacqui, "I was reading about the suites on the boat--they're actually duplexes. They look absolutely huge."

"Well, then, what are you waiting for? Sign me up."

Jacqui smiled and leaned into Algernon. He put his arm around her and kissed her hard and long. After a minute, Jacqui went over to the French doors, closed them and turned the lock. She walked across the room, gave him a 'come hither' signal with her long, skinny finger and went toward a tufted chaise lounge sofa, shedding her clothes along the way. When she got to the chaise she was completely naked and he had to catch up.

Then she smiled, lay back, and said. "Take me, oh noble prince."

Algernon wondered whether that was a line from Shakespeare or Monty Python as he lowered himself down on her.

***

He was smoking an English Oval and had a sheen of sweat on his forehead.

"Just like in the movies, huh?" Jacqui said.

"What do you mean?" Asked Algernon.

"A fag after a shag. Knight would kill me if I let anyone smoke in the house."

"What he doesn't know won't hurt him," Algernon said.

Jacqui laughed. "Nothing can hurt him now," she said, looking away in thought. "So what would you think if I offered you the same job you have, but paid you twice as much as what the Millers pay you."

"How do you know what they're paying me?"

"I have my spies."

"So how much?"

"$125,000," Jacqui said.

Algernon Poole was not *that* easy to get. "Yes, but my Christmas bonus was another $25,000."

"Okay, fine, so make it three hundred thousand," Jacqui said. "And you won't have to wear an evening dress coat and striped trousers like Nancy makes you do. Plus, I promise, I won't refer to you as my *manservant*."

"How very 21st century of you." Algernon stubbed out his Oval in an ashtray that looked as though it had never been used before. "Nancy, or milady as she insists I call her, has been trying to recreate Downton Abbey in that tacky Beaux-Arts Mediterranean house of hers. Which, let me assure you, I can't wait to put that in the rear-view mirror."

"So you accept my offer?"

"Three hundred thousand *and* I get to boff the hot-blooded mistress of the manor," Algernon said. "Are you kidding? No sane man would ever refuse that."

Jacqui leaned forward and kissed him again. "Good," then pulling back, "I have a question for you."

"Ask away."

"How was it that you started life as a duke and ended up in Palm Beach as Nancy Miller's Mr. Carson?"

"First of all, a baron, not a duke. A baron's a little lower on the totem pole."

"But still, royalty."

"Yes, family crest and all. Pip, pip cheerio." Algernon said. "Secondly, I really sucked at finance. Maybe it was because I had a father who couldn't teach me anything but cricket, bridge, gardening, and drinking. But it could have also been that I just had no aptitude for stocks and bonds."

"So you ended up over here--"

"As a highly-remunerated escort," Algernon said.

"So, a gigolo," Jacqui said.

"Yes, but one who drew the line at women over two hundred pounds with three or more chins."

# Ten

The plan was for Crawford to interview Ainsley Buttrick while Ott handled Brewster Collett; then they'd pay another visit to Chuffer Church.

"Wish my parents had been a little more classy," Ott said, as they were going down the elevator at the station.

"What are you talking about?" Crawford asked.

"That last name first name thing," Ott said. "I mean, Brewster or Ainsley…if I had a name like that I probably would have done a lot better with the women in Cleveland. And Charlie, that's just way too common a name."

"You don't think Brewster and Ainsley are a tad pretentious?"

"Maybe a tad," Ott said as they walked out of the building onto South County, "but the only other Mort I knew was this barber on Euclid Avenue."

"That would be a street in the Mistake on the Lake, I take it?"

"Yes, it would be," he said, then shaking his head. "And why do you always have to be so cruel about my beloved hometown, Charlie."

\*\*\*

Brewster Collett was handsome in a blond, blue-eyed, vacuous kind of way. The kind of man who, because he had looks and was a good dancer lured lots of women into bed. He had been born nouveau rich in Lake Forest, Illinois, fifty years ago and his father had the Illinois franchises for both Radio Shack and Blockbuster. That basically meant that, for decades, Brewster didn't have to do anything in the way of gainful employment and so…he didn't. But then in 2010 Blockbuster went bankrupt and five years later, after struggling mightily for years, so did Radio Shack. Collett's father was an inveterate gambler who went to Las Vegas ten times a year, had multiple lavishly-spent-upon mistresses, and had not salted away a dime. Which meant Brewster at the age of fifty was, with the exception of a rent check he got from tenants in a duplex in Lake Bluff, essentially penniless.

Collett had had to downgrade from a house on Coral Lane in Palm Beach to a small Spanish style house in West Palm and hadn't told his friends he'd moved. Instead he'd meet them at the Poinciana, where he was having trouble scraping up the money to pay his annual dues.

***

Ott pushed the doorbell button at the modest house on Greenwood.

Collett came to the door and frowned at the sight of Ott in his brown and orange tie with the big Windsor knot just above his sternum.

"Mr. Collett, my name is Detective Ott," he said. "From the Palm Beach Police Department. I'm investigating the death of Knight Mulcahy in Palm Beach."

Collett made no effort to shake Ott's hand or acknowledge him in any way except as an unseemly blight on his doorstep.

"Ah-huh," he said.

"Yeah, well," Ott said. "May I come in. Ask you a few questions?"

"Yes, sure," said Collett, his eyes still glued to Ott's tie as if there was a big, unsightly turd on it. "Come on in."

Ott walked in and followed Collett into his remarkably unfurnished living room. There was a burgundy Barcalounger facing a big flat screen, a few bamboo chairs without pads, and that was about it.

They sat down in the bamboo chairs, which Ott worried might not support his two hundred and thirty pound heft. Still, he smiled at Collett and took out his pad and pen. "First of all," Ott said. "I just want to confirm that you were at the party given by Knight Mulcahy and his wife three nights ago."

"Yes, yes, I was there," Collett said. "Barely spoke to Knight, though, except to say hello."

Ott nodded. "And did you ever have reason to go outside the house, Mr. Collett?"

Three creases appeared on Collett's forehead. "Why would I?"

"Oh, I don't know, maybe just to get some fresh air or—"

Collett's cell phone rang. He pulled it out and looked at the number. "Oh, got to take this," he said. "Just take a sec."

Ott nodded.

"Hey," Collett said, then turned away and listened.

Ott heard a garbled woman's voice that sounded familiar but he couldn't make out the words.

"Absolutely," Collett said, his eyes lighting up as he glanced down at his watch. "Let's say eight."

Ott listened as hard as he could.

"Yup, Breakers," he said, then in a whisper. "*A bientot, cherie.*"

He clicked off and looked up at Ott. "Sorry, a little business," Collett said. "Now what were you—"

"No problem," Ott said. "So you were inside the whole time at the Mulcahys'?"

"Well, yes," Collett said. "Until I went home."

Ott looked at him like, 'Yeah, well, no shit,' and wrote something on his pad. "And because I've asked everyone this same question: can you think of anyone who might have murdered Knight Mulcahy? You know, a personal or business matter, a grudge, a bad feeling about something, anything at all?"

Collett shook his head slowly, then he stopped as if a thought had intruded, then he looked like he was about to say something, then he started shaking his head again. Then, finally, "Nope. Can't say as I do."

\*\*\*

Crawford found himself in a vast reception room that had as its centerpiece a sculpture of a black panther twice its normal size. It looked like it was either snarling or smiling, Crawford couldn't tell which. The magazine selection there was limited to financial publications, so Crawford was catching up on his emails when Ainsley Buttrick walked in.

"You look like a detective," Buttrick said, examining Crawford's recently purchased Shechers Murilo oxfords with unmasked disdain. "I'm Ainsley Buttrick."

"Mr. Buttrick," Crawford said, standing up and shaking Buttrick's skeletal hand. "Thanks for seeing me—" then pointing to the giant panther next to him—"I like your mascot."

"Thanks," said Buttrick. "It was done by the same sculptor who did the bull up on Wall Street. So come on back and ask me whatever you want."

Crawford followed Buttrick back to a gigantic office with a desk the size of a small aircraft carrier and a conference table off to the side. Buttrick sat down in a chair at the conference table and gestured for Crawford to do the same. Crawford was facing Buttrick's desk, behind which were pictures of Buttrick with both Bush presidents, Mitt Romney, Marco Rubio, Carly Fiorina and the tennis player Roger Federer. Not one Democrat in the bunch.

Buttrick folded his hands, smiled and looked Crawford square in the eyes. "So go ahead, detective, what do you want to know about Knight Mulcahy?"

"Just tell me about your relationship with him, if you would."

"So, as I'm sure you know, Mulcahy was an investor in my fund. He had an inconsequential five million in it and I basically did him a favor by letting him in."

"Five million dollars is inconsequential?"

"Let me amend that," Buttrick said. "It's 'microscopic.' I don't want to sound like a big swingin' dick, but my minimum, as of five years ago, was twenty five million. Knight came to me and practically begged to get in with five."

"But my understanding is, based on his net worth, he could have come up with twenty five million without too much difficulty," Crawford said.

"I know, but he said he was tied up in some illiquid real estate deals and that was all he could do at the time," Buttrick said. "Told me he'd come up with another twenty in six months, but never did."

"Okay, so what happened?" Crawford asked.

"You mean, why'd he go spouting off about the big black cat?"

"Yeah," Crawford said. "Is that what you call it?"

"Some reporter at the *Wall Street Journal* came up with that," Buttrick said. "I kinda liked it."

"Okay, so as I understand it, Mulcahy had some losses in… *the big black cat*," Crawford said. "And chose his radio show as a forum to—"

"—trash me," Buttrick said, getting more animated. "He lost about as much as I win on a typical golf bet, then goes off on the cat, saying it's a big loser. Well, if it's such a big loser then how come I'm worth 6.7 billion dollars?"

Crawford didn't know the answer. "What was your response to him, saying what he said about your fund on his radio show?"

Buttrick smiled. "My first response was to go ballistic, I won't lie to you, I was really pissed. My second response was to sue the shit out of the guy because of a confidentiality agreement he signed. But my third response was—" he shrugged his shoulders, "not to give a rat's ass. Know why?"

Crawford shook his head.

"'Cause of the guy's audience," Buttrick said. "Bunch of rednecks from Arkansas pulling down 30K a year. Them hearing about Mulcahy losing money in a hedge fund…. 'What the hell's a hedge fund?' they're wondering."

It was a good point.

"Mulcahy's money was inconsequential," Buttrick went on. "So you see, detective, the concept of me going down to his beach house with a gun when he's down there getting his rocks off with some bimbo is about as absurd as one of his listeners putting cash in the cat."

On that note, Crawford got to his feet. "Thank you, Mr. Buttrick, I appreciate your time."

He didn't see the need to shake Buttrick's bony hand again.

"You're very welcome, detective," Buttrick said, then a smile. "If you're ever looking for a place to put that paycheck of yours...."

Yuk-yuk-yuk.

***

Twenty minutes later, Crawford and Ott were walking up the steps to Chuffer Church's house.

"So you didn't even ask Collett about his relationship with Jacqui Mulcahy?" Crawford asked.

"No," said Ott. "I thought about it, but then figured, what's the point? He'd just deny it. Even though he took her call in the middle of our conversation. Pretty sure it was her, anyway. I was really just trying to get a sense whether the man could kill somebody or not."

"And?"

"No fucking way," Ott said. "Guy totally lacks motivation."

"What are you talking about," Crawford said, pressing the doorbell. "You told me the guy was broke. Needed a meal ticket, i.e., Jacqui Mulcahy. Ever heard of the saying, starvation is motivation?"

"Can't say as I have."

"'Cause I just made it up."

"I figured," Ott said, pressing the doorbell.

***

Crawford and Ott were in Chuffer Church's living room again. The paintings and the furniture were all awash in pastel colors, as if Lily Pulitzer herself had been turned loose with a holster of yellow, pink, blue, and green paintbrushes.

"Mr. Church," Crawford said, sitting across from him in a wicker chair, "we came up with a few discrepancies in your story. About where you were the night Knight Mulcahy was killed."

Church looked offended. "What are you talking about," he said. "I told you we watched a movie here, then--"

"Actually," Ott cut in, "we have a time-dated video which shows your car coming out of your driveway at exactly--"

"Okay, okay," Church said quickly. "But what's the big deal?"

"The big deal is we don't expect you to lie to us," Crawford said.

"Which, clearly, you did," Ott added.

Chuffer Church inspected the tops of his Testonis as if there was a secret message etched into them.

"So, the question is, where exactly did you go?" Crawford asked, impatiently.

"This place over in West Palm," Church mumbled.

"A restaurant? A bar? What was it?" Ott asked. "We're going to need to confirm that you actually went there this time."

"It's called Claudia's," Church said.

"The strip joint?" Ott said.

Crawford stifled a laugh.

"It's a gentleman's club," said Church.

"Oh, sorry," Ott said, struggling to keep a straight face.

"I met a guy there," Church said. "We had business to discuss."

"And how long were you there?" Crawford asked.

"About two hours," said Church.

"So someone would be able to confirm you were there?" Ott asked. "A bartender maybe, the bouncer... or --" he couldn't resist-- "one of those scantily-clad ladies who dances with poles?"

Church looked offended. "I was just there to meet a man and discuss a business venture."

Church reminded Crawford of the man who claimed to buy *Playboy* for the articles.

"So who was it you met with?" Ott asked.

"His name is Jabbah Al-Jabbah," Church said. "Name ring a

bell?"

Crawford and Ott both shook their heads. "Can't say it does," Crawford said.

"The royal family of Saudi Arabia," Church said, looking pleased to throw around the title.

"Okay," Crawford said. "So, if you don't mind, what was the business meeting about?"

"It's really none of your business," Church said. "But I'll tell you anyway, since I have nothing to hide. Then we can be done with this whole ridiculous conversation. I've been talking to Mr. Al-Jabbah about becoming a backer in a business of mine."

"Oh, you mean, CC Ryder?" Ott said.

Church's mouth went into a wide O. "How is it possible you know the name of my company?"

"I keep an eye on the fashion scene," Ott said.

Church looked quizzical.

"Actually I been checking up on you a little. Stores in New York, Boston and LA, right?"

"Yeah, and about to be five more," Church said. "Including one here."

"Congratulations," Crawford said. "So you went straight from your house to Claudia's?"

"Yup, in the opposite direction of Knight Mulcahy's, I might add."

Crawford knew Ott would check security cameras south of Church's house to confirm that.

Crawford looked at Ott. Ott shrugged. It was a wrap.

"Well, thank you, Mr. Church," Crawford stood up and shook Church's hand.

Ott did the same. "Look forward to getting my first pair of pink pants at your new store," he said.

Church didn't realize he was kidding. "We'll have some fantastic bow ties, too. You'd look good in a bowtie, detective."

# Eleven

Just to keep track of all his suspects, Crawford wrote down their names on a white board in his office. Then beside each name he wrote a short description. Beside Jacqui Mulcahy, he wrote '$.' Beside Paul Mulcahy, he wrote 'ditto.' Beside Brewster Collett, he wrote, 'wants Jackie.' Beside Lila Moline, he wrote 'wants Knight.' Beside Chuffer Church, he wrote 'business deal went south.' Beside Ainsley Buttirick, he wrote 'Knight trashed fund.' Beside Sam Pratt, he wrote 'golf cheater?' Beside Ned Durrell he wrote, 'writer-fight with Knight.' He knew he was forgetting a few. Oh, yeah, Skagg Magwood and Earl Hardin. Beside their names, he wrote '?' And finally, he wrote 'John/Bob,' and next to it, 'MIDBBB'—which stood for the man in the double-breasted blue blazer. God, he hoped he hadn't forgotten anybody.

Right after that he got a call from the medical examiner, Bob Hawes, a guy he had a short but rancorous history with. Hawes stated emphatically that Knight Mulcahy had been killed between 9:40 and 9:45 on the night of his party. Crawford started to say that it was impossible to be so exact, but let it go. Why get into it with the guy, yet again?

He was now on his way down to the basement of the station house where the evidence techs kept their offices.

Dominica McCarthy was talking on her cell.

She spotted him and motioned him over. "We'll be there at 2," she said. "Does that work?" She nodded, then said, "Okay, see you then," and hung up.

"Hey, Charlie," she said, raising her palms in mock protest: "You don't call, you don't write."

"Sorry," he said, "you know how it is when I got a homicide."

She sighed. "Yeah, only too well. 'Bye-bye, Dominica, see you just as soon as I solve this sucker.' Which could be years."

Crawford laughed. "Don't be a wiseass. And those are both big exaggerations. But at least you recognize I eventually get my man."

"Yup. Just like the Mounties," She said as her cell phone rang. She ignored it.

Dominica was the second of Crawford's Palm Beach girlfriends, something they kept under wraps. He had sworn off women for a while after the rough break-up of his seven-year marriage up in New York. But then along came Lil Fonseca. A blond knockout. Ambitious. Scheming. Conniving. It had been a short, but rousing run. Then came Dominica. Beautiful brown eyes, bouncy, full hair, uncomplicated, not to mention a figure everyone agreed was way above average. He had fallen hard for her, but now its status was on-again, off-again.

"What's your batting average since you've been down here? Four for four," she asked.

"Come on, girl, you forgot one. Five for five." Crawford gave her a fake fist-pump. "Hey, look, I came here to take you out to lunch. So quit givin' me a hard time."

Dominica started nodding. "Uh-huh. To discuss Knight Mulcahy's murder, right?"

"Among other things," he said. "Also, to catch up with you. Find out how Hobo's doin, how your surfing's comin' along. You know, what's new in your life?"

"Hobo's still eating my shoes and I got a new short board."

"Sorry about the shoes, but that's great about the board. What kind?"

Dominica shook her head and smiled. "Like you know the names of surf boards."

"True."

"So you got the small talk out of the way," Dominica said. "Want to talk about Mulcahy now?"

Crawford shuffled awkwardly. "Come on," he said, "are you trying to make me feel like a guy with an agenda? I mean, here I am trying to take you out to lunch and you're making it sound like I'm just one big ulterior-motive guy."

"Hey, you said it," Dominica held up a hand. "But I don't hold it against you."

"Okay, okay, let's go," he said. "Before I ask Cato out instead."

"She'd kill to get the invite from you, lover boy."

Green's Pharmacy on North County didn't sound like a lunch place, but it made one of the best hamburgers in Palm Beach. Best breakfast, too. Crawford liked it because it was right across from St. Edward's church. So he could hit mass on Sunday, then slide across the street and do a swiss cheese omelette with a couple of big, greasy sausages and rye toast slathered with strawberry jam.

Crawford and Dominica sat down and a waitress came right over.

"Hi, I'll have the chef salad," Dominica said to the waitress, "can you chop it up?"

"Sure," the waitress answered. "I can do any damn thing you want."

The waitresses at Green's, who wouldn't dream of allowing themselves to be called the more contemporary term--wait staff--had a certain amount of pressure on them. Not only to crank out good food in a timely fashion, but also to be bantering good 'ol gals, right out of some TV show with an annoying laugh track. That's the way it had always been at Green's.

Dominica was still looking over the menu. "Actually, you know what," she said. "I'll have the clam chowder instead."

"Sure," said the waitress, "chop it up?"

Dominica laughed. "Just a side of Saltines."

Crawford went with his go-to: burger n' fries. "So far this case is just a lot of interviews going nowhere," he grumbled. "I might as well get out a telephone book--if they still had 'em--and go through it one by one."

"So you don't have any primaries?"

"That's the problem, I got too many," Crawford said, putting the menu down. "Knight Mulcahy wasn't a guy who was gonna win a lot of popularity contests. He pissed off a lot of people. No, let me amend that, he pissed off everyone he came in contact with."

"Didn't seem to hurt his ratings," Dominica said.

"I know, most popular talk show in the universe," Crawford said. "But, it's funny, in the town where he lived, seems like nobody could stand the guy."

Dominica frowned. "That's kinda sad."

"Yeah," Crawford said. "Didn't even have a Labrador retriever that loved him."

The waitress showed up with their food.

"That was fast," he said.

She nodded. "Saw you park your car," she said. "Had the burger on the grill before you walked in."

Crawford gave her a thumbs-up and took a bite of his burger. "God, that's good," he said, then he put it down. "You know what's really amazing?"

"What's that?"

"How much cheating goes on in this town."

Dominica chuckled. "Jesus, where'd that come from?"

"I was just thinking. I mean, seems like everyone cheats," he said. "Mulcahy--so my CI tells me--had at least three girlfriends, his wife

ditto--"

"You mean, boyfriends?"

"Yeah, but who knows?"

"Who else?"

"Who else what?"

"Is in this cheater file of yours?"

"I don't know, just about everybody," Crawford said.

"I wonder if it's a rich persons thing," Dominica said.

"Maybe," Crawford said. "Not like I've done a survey. I'd say it's more like an idleness thing?"

"Meaning too much time on your hands, why not fuck around?"

"Yeah, something like that," Crawford said. "I'm working on another theory, too."

"Care to run it by me?"

"Okay," Crawford said, "but it's not fully developed yet."

Dominica shrugged.

"So a lot of people here have like these massive Trump-size egos—"

"No argument there."

"And I think people like that feel they deserve everything they can get their hot little hands on-- money, power, sex--"

"The big three, huh?" Dominica said, nodding. "I think you might be on to something, Charlie."

"Yeah, I'm always on to something. Question is, is it relevant to finding a murderer or not?" he said, then he had another thought. "Also, another thing I've noticed is, it's everywhere."

"What's everywhere?"

"Well, they're so many single women in this town, you know, hustling to make a buck—nannies, baby sitters, real-estate agents, women who work at the shops—hell, for all I know, maybe even evidence-tech babes, and no shortage of men chasing them."

"Not this evidence-tech babe, my friend."

"But you know what I mean, men figure every woman is fair game."

"I'm not sure Palm Beach has a monopoly on that."

"Probably right. I just see these really old codgers squiring around women who look like they could be their granddaughters."

"Maybe they are."

Crawford shook his head.

"How do you know?"

"By the look in their eyes," Crawford said. "The look of lust."

Dominica, in the middle of a spoonful of chowder, stifled a laugh and swallowed. "I think you're starting to lose it, Charlie. You need a nice, long vacation."

"Sounds good," he said. "Where you want to go."

"You know you're not going anywhere until you're six for six," she said. "And so on that note, let's get back to Mulcahy."

Crawford nodded. "You got nothing at the scene, right?"

"Not true," Dominica said. "I got hair, I got fibers. But who knows who they belong to. Could be Mulcahy, could be his wife, could be his son, could be the cleaning lady."

"And when will you get the results?"

"Day after tomorrow."

"What about the two bullets?"

"You have to ask Hawes."

Crawford put his hamburger down. "So, are we on the same page? Mulcahy was having sex, then the woman left and a guy who followed 'em down popped him."

Dominica chewed that over for a second. "Yeah, sounds right. But maybe they were a team?"

Crawford started nodding. "Never thought of that."

Dominica tapped her finger on the table a few times. "She sets it up. The guy finishes it off," she said. "Or a husband or a boyfriend catches 'em in the act. Or, hey, maybe it was a guy."

"What do you mean?"

"Maybe he was having sex with a guy," Dominica shrugged. "It happens, you know."

"Yeah, I know, but from everything I know about Mulcahy he was the most heterosexual guy on the planet."

Dominica reached for a packet of Saltines. "Didn't they use to say that about Rock Hudson?"

Crawford nodded. "Good point."

"Or, I gotta another one, maybe he was having sex with a woman and she plugged him 'cause he was a shitty--"

Crawford put his hand up to her mouth. "Okay, Dominica, I think you're getting a little carried away now."

She laughed. "I know, I know, 'just stick to hair and fibers, right?'"

# TWELVE

Crawford knew a man who was a member of the Poinciana Club he could *almost* call a friend. His name was David Balfour and he was what used to be known as a playboy. Not that the term had disappeared, it just had a certain dated quality to it. Like if you Googled 'playboy,' there'd be a line-up of guys from the '80's with long sideburns, tight shirts unbuttoned down to their navel, maybe a gold chain or two, standing next to a Maserati convertible.

Balfour had actually been quite helpful in Crawford's previous cases, and they had a joke between them that Balfour was Crawford's C.I.—meaning confidential informer. Fact was, Balfour's information had definitely helped solve two of those cases. Crawford suspected that the C.I. designation actually gave Balfour a sense of purpose, since most of his days consisted of more frivolous pursuits like chasing women and deciding between going to the happy hour at the Breakers or the one at Ta-boo.

Balfour had asked Crawford several times to be his guest at the Poinciana for a round of golf, but Crawford had begged off, saying his game was not up to Poinciana standards. And though he had been a seven handicap up north, Crawford hadn't played more than a handful of times since moving to Florida. That was at the muni golf course with a motley crew that wore cargo shorts and day-glo Under Armour t-shirts and lugged around six-packs of beer in their bags. Crawford had also always felt that, as a cop, he should keep his distance from men he might have to arrest one day. And, for that reason, he stayed away from bars, parties, and country-club golf courses on Palm Beach island.

But now might be the time to break his rule and take Balfour up on his offer to play golf at the Poinciana—get a first-hand look at where Knight Mulcahy spent so much time and, apparently, created so many enemies. It also would be eye-opening to get a close-up peek at a few of the case's many suspects.

According to Rose Clarke, Sam Pratt, Chuffer Church, Ainsley

Buttrick and Knight Mulcahy's son Paul were all Poinciana members. He had a hunch he might be able to dig up even more members there, who might have had a motive to kill Mulcahy.

He dialed Balfour's cell.

It was just past two PM. He knew Balfour's schedule pretty well by now. His combination chef/ housekeeper prepared him lunch at one o'clock--usually something on the healthy side. To accompany lunch, Balfour would always mix himself a Bullshot--a drink which consisted of a good slug of Tito's vodka, ice, V-8 juice, beef bouillon, Worcestershire sauce, a heavy jolt of Tabasco, then another shot of Tito's, which Balfour called a floater.

The idea of a Bullshot had its appeal to Crawford, but whenever Balfour offered him one, he politely refused. "On the job, huh?" Balfour would say, and Crawford always nodded. Balfour explained that he kept it to two Bullshots, having cut back from three five years before. He described how, back then, his routine was to knock back three stiff ones, then go out to his pool and nod off--essentially pass out--in one of his heavily-padded chaise lounges. One time, he explained, he ended up with a particularly bad sunburn. Not only that, he explained, it also turned out to be a waste of a perfectly good afternoon, which could otherwise have been spent playing eighteen holes, a game of backgammon with the boys, or a tryst with one of his many lady friends.

"Hey, Charlie, long time no talk, what's up?"

"How you been, David?"

"Great, man, just sitting here pool-side with a libation and my friend, Alexa."

Of course.

"Well, I won't keep you," Crawford said. "Hey, I wondered if that offer to play golf at the Poinciana was still open?"

"Damn right it is," Balfour said enthusiastically. "Just so happens I had a guy drop out of my foursome tomorrow morning. Can you play then?"

Tomorrow was Saturday. "Sure. What time?"

"Nine fifteen."

"Perfect. I'll be there."

"All right, finally," Balfour said. "Our chance to go drown a few golf balls together."

"Looking forward to it," Crawford said. "Should I come a little early… hit a few out on the range?"

"Yeah, absolutely, make it a quarter of."

"See you then."

***

Crawford had a full dance card that afternoon. He and Ott were meeting the novelist Ned Durrell at two, the antique shop owner Lila Moline at three, then he was having a 'working drink' with Rose Clarke right after that.

Crawford had also learned that there'd been a photographer from the *Glossy*--the nickname for The Palm Beach *Daily Standard*-- at the Mulcahy party, who he also wanted to hook up with. The way he heard it, Knight was apparently opposed to any photographic record of his nocturnal shenanigans, but socially ambitious Jacqui felt that a little pictorial documentation of her gamboling with Palm Beach's movers and shakers couldn't hurt. And Jacqui, ultimately, had worn Knight down.

So Crawford had gone to the *Glossy* offices and met with the photographer, who was only too happy to show Crawford the pictures he had taken. Crawford suspected that if something came of the photographs he was shown, the photographer might make the claim that he was instrumental in helping solve the murder.

It took Crawford more than an hour to go through all the photographer's pictures. He concentrated on the ones of Knight with his guests. One with Ned Durrell caught his attention because Durrell had a deep-creased frown as he and Mulcahy stood face-to-face like two boxers in the ring about to go at it. Crawford's other read was that it looked as if Mulcahy had either just emitted a noxious odor or, in keeping with his reputation, had just unloaded a barrage of invective at the novelist.

There were also several pictures of Knight with a good-looking redhead that caught Crawford's attention. One, in particular, showed Knight and the redhead going out the back French doors. Then he realized that it was probably the woman Paul Mulcahy had mentioned. The one who had come back in with Knight a few minutes later. Knight was turned in such a way that it looked like he was trying not to get spotted as he made his exit. Crawford made a mental note to ask Paul Mulcahy if the woman he saw his father leave with was the red-head.

Then Crawford had thought to ask the photographer if he knew who the woman was.

"Yeah, that's Olivia Griswold." The photog leaned closer and whispered, "AKA the red menace."

He remembered that was the name Paul Mulchay had said. He planned to ask Rose Clarke what the derivation of the nickname was. She probably had several juicy footnotes on the matter.

The photographer had claimed he had more pictures at his house in West Palm and asked if Crawford wanted to follow him over there to see them. Crawford thanked him, said that he had to be somewhere soon, and asked him to bring them in to the *Glossy's* office the next day. The photographer assured him he would. Then Crawford asked him if it would be all right if he took a few of the pictures and the photographer said he had proofs of all of them and gave him the ones he wanted.

***

Crawford swung by the station house and picked up Ott for the Ned Durrell interview. Durrell lived in a big house on Barton. Crawford had heard him referred to as the "poor man's James Patterson"--also, a Palm Beach resident and a writer who cranked out a million bestsellers in production-line fashion.

Durrell wrote spy novels that featured a snobbish, Gauloise-smoking French aristocrat as its protagonist. That was about all Crawford knew because he had bogged down after slogging through two sluggish chapters in his one and only attempt to get through one called *Night*-something.

Durrell greeted them with a suspicious look and a snarly poodle at his feet. The poodle was making noises like it had a bone caught in its throat and was trying to work it free.

"Thanks for seeing us, Mr. Durrell," Crawford said, putting out his hand. "I'm Detective Crawford, and my partner, Detective Ott."

Durrell shook their hands limply. "Come on in," he said, stepping back inside.

Crawford and Ott following him in, through the foyer and into a room off the back of the living room. It was clearly where Durrell knocked out his quasi-bestsellers. There were eight framed covers of his novels on the wall behind his Herman Miller Eames chair.

Durrell walked to his chair and motioned to the two chairs opposite it.

"Have a seat," he said, like he wanted to get it over with fast.

Crawford and Ott sat.

Facing the eight covers, Crawford thought about coming up with something complimentary about *Night* whatever, but knew he'd be pretty bad at faking it.

"Mr. Durrell," he said. "As part of our investigation, we're going around talking to as many friends of Knight Mulcahy as we can."

Durrell put his hands together, then looked up. "Knight and I barely tolerated each other, but go ahead."

Crawford nodded. Like Rose Clarke, blunt was the word that came to mind.

"We have a photo of you two talking," said Crawford, taking it out of his breast pocket.

Ott glanced down at it. "Now that you mention it, Mr. Durrell," he said, "it does kinda look like two people who barely tolerated each other."

Once in a while, Crawford felt like he should apologize for

Ott, but his comment didn't seem to faze Durrell, who seemed lost in thought.

"He said on the air that my latest book--which is up for a Macavity Award, by the way--was, in so many words, a piece of shit," Durrell said.

Crawford didn't know what a Macavity Award was but was pretty sure it fell short of a Pulitzer.

"So is that what your conversation was about?" Crawford asked, remembering now that it was called *Night Wolf*.

"Yeah, brief and acrimonious," Durrell said. "He went out of his way to tell his audience, well, actually he cleaned it up, said it was 'a piece of steaming excrement.' You know, he could have just kept it to himself, how he felt. I mean, we do live in the same town. Bump into each other at Publix and shit."

"Gotta say, one bad review doesn't strike me as much of a reason to kill a guy," Ott said.

"Well, thank you, detective, for weighing in," Durrell said, then frowned almost as deeply as in the photo. "Wait, you came here 'cause I'm a suspect?"

"As I said," Crawford said, "we're talking to half the town."

"You seem pretty well plugged in, Mr. Durrell," Ott said. "Anybody you can think of who might have had a motive to kill Mulcahy?"

Durrell exhaled.

"No, I really don't have a clue," Durrell said. "And if I did, I wouldn't tell you. You know why?"

"Why?" Ott said.

"'Cause it would probably come back to bite me in the ass."

"Why's that?" Ott asked.

"Because you'd go to whoever and say, 'This author told us you had a motive to kill Knight Mulca--"

"That would be kind of a bush move," Ott cut in. "We treat everything we hear as strictly confidential."

"Whatever," said Durrell. "Fact is, I have absolutely no idea who killed Knight Mulcahy except it wasn't me. Kinda glad he's not around to call my next book a piece of shit, though."

# Thirteen

Lila Moline was too Audrey Hepburn-ish for Crawford. Classically beautiful with dark straight hair, prominent cheekbones and striking brown eyes, but a little frail, a little brittle, not enough meat on the bone for him.

Crawford could tell Ott was smitten, though. For one thing, he was on his best behavior. He wasn't throwing around zinger lines meant to catch someone off guard, no 'gotchas,' or 'Ott-chas' as Crawford called them.

Norm Rutledge, head of Palm Beach PD, had once given Ott a stern lecture about cleaning up his Q & A. "This is Palm Beach, you know," Rutledge had said to him, "not fucking Cleveland"—where Ott had spent twenty two years staring down at stiffs on the snow-covered streets.

Crawford was nibbling around the edges, working his way up to a direct question about Moline's relationship with Knight Mulcahy as they stood at the counter of Moline's shop, Les Trucs, on North County Way. Moline was facing them, nobody else was in the shop. To Crawford it felt like one of those places which--on a good day-- had a grand total of twenty customers come through its doors. The kind of place where you went when you were looking for something very specific, or just wanted to kill a half hour.

"So Mr. and Mrs. Mulcahy were old friends of yours?" Crawford asked.

"I've known them both for quite a while," Moline said. "As you know, Palm Beach is a small town."

Ott nodded thoughtfully.

"It's come to our attention," Crawford said, "that you might have been having a relationship with Mr. Mulcahy."

Ott gave him a look like, 'Nice and delicate, Charlie.'

But to Crawford's surprise, Moline didn't flinch. She just sighed. "You'll never quote me, right?"

"Never," said Crawford as he and Ott shook their heads in unison. "That's not how we do things."

"Okay, the reality is Knight and Jacqui had kind of an open marriage," Moline said. "I mean, they didn't call it that but that's what it was."

Crawford and Ott waited for more.

"Knight asked me out for dinner once when Jacqui was out of town," she said. "He was a rich and powerful man and I was flattered. Except he took me to this complete dive in--of all places-- Riviera Beach. So, long story short, we had an affair. Only problem was--as I soon found out--he was having affairs with half the women in Palm Beach."

"Like who else?" Crawford asked.

Moline sighed again. "I'm not going to say. I just know he was. I mean, there was even talks of orgies. I didn't even know they were still around."

Ott who was taking notes looked up. "Really? Orgies?"

"I don't know," Moline said with a shrug. "Nobody ever asked me to one."

A few minutes later Crawford and Ott thanked Lila Moline and went in different directions.

*** 

Crawford was ten minutes late for his "working drink" with Rose Clarke. She was talking to the bartender at Mookie's when Crawford got there. He had suggested they go to a bar in Citiplace at first but she said she'd rather go to the place that Crawford had once mentioned to her: his cop bar in West Palm.

Soak up some local color, she said.

You mean, go slumming, he said.

Whatever you want to call it, she said.

He came up behind her as she and Jack Scarsiola, the owner and bartender, seemed to be deep into it.

"He tellin' you about his heroic exploits back in the good ol' days," Crawford said, flicking his head at Scarsiola, a former West Palm Beach cop.

Rose swung around and smiled. "Hey, Charlie," she said. "No, about some barroom brawl you had in here."

Not one of Crawford's prouder moments. "I don't recall," he said.

Scarsiola burst out laughing. "Come on, you remember," he said. "You were Mike Tyson that night."

Crawford flicked his head. "Let's go sit at a table."

Scarsiola went to the tap and drew up a beer as Rose followed Crawford over to the table.

"Mike Tyson, huh?"

"Don't listen to that guy," Crawford said as he pulled out her chair.

"Bet you're the only guy in this place who does that."

"Does what?"

"Pulls out a chair for a woman."

"Don't be a snob, Rose," Crawford said. "All cops go to charm school."

She laughed as Crawford sat down and Scarsiola brought over his Bud draft.

"Devastating uppercut," Scarsiola muttered with a wink.

"Can it, Scar," Crawford said as Scarsiola walked away.

"Come on, Charlie, us girls love to hear about tough, macho guys," Rose said.

"Sorry, but that ain't me," he said, taking a sip of his Bud. "So how's business."

"Sucks," she said. "I had two contracts fall through this week."

"Which means you only make 3 mil this year instead of 4?"

Rose laughed and took a sip of her wine. "Nah, more than that," she said. "By the way, this wine isn't half bad."

"Meaning it's a quarter bad?"

"No, meaning it's pretty good," Rose said.

"Well, good. You didn't think I'd bring you to a place that sold swill, did you?"

She leaned across the table and gave him a kiss on the cheek. "Never."

Crawford reached into the breast pocket of his jacket. "So I brought a bunch of photos that were taken at Knight Mulcahy's party."

He handed her the stack and she started going through them.

"Ned Durrell," she said, shaking her head, "what a dick. You ever read one of his books?"

Crawford shook his head. "Not all the way."

"Writes sex scenes like he's never had sex before."

"That wouldn't be Knight Mulcahy's problem."

"No, sure wouldn't."

"He ever go after—"

Rose looked up and smiled. "Yes, and I had absolutely no interest. Yuck."

"Just checking."

"I don't remember seeing the man in the double-breasted blue blazer there that night," Rose said pointing.

"Let's see," Crawford said eagerly.

Rose handed him the picture, but the man was cut off above the chin.

"And you said his name might be John?"

Rose nodded. "I think so."

"'Cause someone else thought it was Bob."

"I don't know for sure," Rose said. "Know what's kinda creepy?"

"What's that?"

"That somebody in one of these pictures is Knight Mulcahy's killer."

Crawford nodded. "Except maybe not everyone who was there is in these pictures."

Rose nodded and scanned the room. "Can we talk about something other than Knight Mulcahy's murder now?"

"Sure," Crawford said. "What do you want to talk about?"

Rose thought for a second. "Why you're so obsessed with your job? I mean, I'm really into mine, too, but I've never seen anyone like you."

Crawford shrugged. "I don't really know the answer."

Rose shook her head. "Yeah, you do. Come on."

"Because I have no life?"

"You could if you wanted," Rose raised her hand for a waiter. "This conversation calls for another drink."

"Ah, sorry, aren't any waiters here, kid." Crawford stood. "Same thing?"

"I don't know," she said, looking at her empty wine glass, "how about something with a little rum in it?"

"I got just the ticket," Crawford said, as he turned toward the bar.

Three minutes later he was back with two dark-colored drinks with limes floating in them.

"So whaddaya got there?" Rose asked. "Looks kinda lethal."

'Meyers and OJ with a big hunka lime," Crawford said. "A health drink, you might call it."

Rose laughed. "Oh, is it now? How come it's so dark? Must be about 75% Meyers."

"Nah, only two-thirds."

Rose laughed. "You tryin' to get me drunk or something? So you can take advantage of me?"

"I thought you wanted me to tell you why I have no life,"

Crawford said, taking a hefty pull on his rum drink. "Ah, nectar of the Gods."

"So? Why don't you? Have a life, that is. You're definitely a workaholic... right?"

He took another long pull and looked at his half-filled glass. "I'd say I'm definitely some kinda 'holic.'"

"Seriously, I want to hear," Rose said, taking a more restrained sip.

Crawford shrugged. "I don't know, I don't seem to do much besides work anymore," he said. "I used to love to play sports. Go to the occasional art gallery even. Saw lotsa movies. Now I just run around after guys who kill people."

"I have an idea," Rose said, wiping her lips with a cocktail napkin.

"You always do."

"Maybe you should get into a relationship," Rose said. "Something where it's not all about you chasing guys who kill people, but more about doing stuff with someone else. You know, the ol' 'sharing your life with someone' concept. You've heard of that, right, Charlie?"

He had certainly teed that one up for her.

"Got any idea about who might be a candidate for this, 'sharing my life with?'"

"Don't be a jerk, Charlie," she said. "Not necessarily me, though that would be a damn good choice, but there are lots of women out there...."

He waited.

She tapped her fingers on the table a few times, then looked up. "But clearly you couldn't do any better than me."

He took another sip of his drink, more moderate this time. "The question is, could you do better than me?" he said. "And I think the answer to that is a definite *yes*."

# Fourteen

Jabbah Al-Jabbah was sitting at a Starbucks a block away from the mosque in Lake Worth. With him were Bashir El-Nadal and Habib Hamdi. Bashir had been born Jamie Deering and Habib, Deshawn Brown. Bashir had grown up in a middle-class, white neighborhood, loved tennis as a kid, and wanted to make a career of it, but he didn't have a big serve and his net game was only so-so. Nevertheless, he had borrowed his new Muslim name from his tennis idol, Rafael Nadal. He thought Nadal had kind of a Muslim ring to it.

Deshawn came from a desperately poor black family, with no father in the picture, and had dropped out of school halfway through tenth grade.

Bashir and Habib both wore thobes, long, loose white robes that hung down to their ankles. Bashir's had a stain at the right elbow from changing the oil on his Nissan Altima.

Al-Jabbah, a fifty one year old man from the Saudi Arabian royal family, was wearing a black wool bisht over his thobe, which indicated superior rank.

Four men in work clothes had shot threatening glances at them when they walked in. Muslims weren't exactly welcomed with open arms anywhere in Lake Worth, Florida. Things had gotten much worse after the Paris massacre, then the slaughter of the fourteen people in San Bernadino, California a few days later, and finally when Trump said no Muslims should be let into the country. A few days after Trump's edict, someone had thrown a pig's head at the mosque in Lake Worth and someone else, or maybe the same person, had made a call with a profanity-laced warning that the mosque was going to get fire-bombed.

Al-Jabbah, a man with a formidably intimidating glare, just stared back at the four rednecks. He was giving them his 'don't fuck with me' look, which seemed to further imply, 'cause you have no idea who you're messin' with.'

Al-Jabbah slid two hundred-dollar bills across the table to Bashir, then did the same to Habib.

"This is for the shooting range," Al-Jabbah said. "I want you both to spend many hours there, perfecting your marksmanship."

"This won't go very far," Bashir said. "That place is really expensive."

Habib nodded in agreement.

Al-Jabbah reached in his pocket, pulled out four more hundred-dollar bills and slid them across the table. "That's enough to make you into sharpshooters."

Bashir nodded and leaned into Al-Jabbah. "So…can you tell us what our fatwa is going to be?"

Al-Jabbah ignored Bashir's misuse of the word. He knew perfectly well what Bashir was asking.

"Just learn how to shoot straight," Al-Jabbah hissed. "I will let you know *when* you need to know."

Bashir smiled and said, a little too loudly for Al-Jabbah. "Don't worry, my brother, we'll be able to take out a whole school in five minutes after a coupla weeks there."

Al-Jabbah leaned forward, his nostrils flaring. "*Never, ever* again say anything like that in a public place. Do you understand me?"

Bashir, rebuked, nodded and lowered his eyes.

Al-Jabbah looked around to see if anyone might have heard what Bashir said.

Satisfied that no one had, he stood up.

"I will see you at the mosque," he said. "As-Salaam-Alaikum."

"As-Salaam-Alaikum."

"As-Salaam-Alaikum."

***

Al-Jabbah drove his Bentley Continental GT Speed Coupe to the Royal & Alien Club on North Lake Way in Palm Beach. He knew that he had done the right thing reading the riot act to slid into his flip-flops and walked down to the lobby, then out onto the street.

Jeanelle, the smiley one with the gold tooth, took his order at Dunkin' Donuts. His usual: two blueberry donuts and a medium extra-dark coffee.

He took the coffee and two donuts, got a paper from the blue metal box and went over to "his" table. The Palm Beach *Post* was, at most, a ten-minute read but today he thought it might stretch out to at least fifteen. It was the fourth day after Knight Mulcahy's murder and there was still a lot of mileage to be had by reporters dredging up Mulcahy's colorful, and somewhat sordid, past. Not to mention, speculation about what might have been the motive to kill him. The subhead to the main Mulcahy story, which was battling it out with another one entitled, "Fake Kid Doc Arrested Again," was "Cops Down to a Handful of Suspects." Oh, really, thought Crawford, and just who might they be? He scanned down with interest and by the third paragraph had found no names. "A high-powered local businessman" was referred to, as was a "Washington politician who had clashed repeatedly with Mulcahy." Crawford had no clue who the Washington politician might be, but thought Ainsley Buttrick, Chuffer Church, and Brewster Collett all fit the description of high-powered local businessmen, even though, in reality, Collett fell quite a bit short.

He got to the end of the article and realized that it was just a rehash of the last three days' articles and a lot of it seemed to be pure fiction.

Then he went to the sports page--sped through it in about a minute, mainly reading headlines--and thought about his upcoming golf game at the Poinciana. The main thing was not to embarrass himself too badly. He assumed David Balfour was good, since it seemed he spent a substantial portion of his life playing or practicing. Crawford had also observed two shelves in Balfour's library dedicated to the display of silver trophies, along with cups and bowls of varying shapes and sizes, which seemed to be for winning tournaments, or at the very least, coming in second. Crawford finished up the last bite of his second blueberry donut, then washed it down with a final sip of coffee and stood up to go.

He walked back to his apartment, took a shower, changed into golf clothes and drove over to the Poinciana.

*** 

David Balfour was waiting for him at the driving range. Balfour wore dark blue shorts, a blue and white Polo shirt and brown alligator golf shoes that looked expensive. He was around fifty, had the hard belly of a guy who did a lot of sit-ups and Caesar salads, and topped off the whole presentation with perfect, brown fluffy hair without a trace of grey.

He eyeballed Crawford's golf clubs skeptically. "A Nike Sasquatch, huh?" referring to Crawford's 8-year old, oversized yellow driver. "Thought that went out with neon orange golf balls?"

That was news to Crawford, who had three of the orange balls in his bag. "They're not around anymore?"

Balfour just smiled and shook his head.

A guy on the other side of Balfour, hitting wedge shots, swung around and checked out Crawford with skepticism.

"Charlie, this is Earl Hardin," Balfour said, turning to the man. "One of the guys playing with us."

"Hey, Earl, nice to meet you," Crawford said, remembering the name from when he and Ott had questioned Skagg Magwood. Magwood had been vague about his connection to Mulcahy.

Hardin gave Crawford a cursory nod.

Balfour turned back to Crawford and said under his breath. "Helluva good player. Takes his game a little too seriously, though."

"I heard that, Balfour," Hardin said, then turned to Crawford. "Haven't seen you around before, you an out-of-town member?"

Crawford thumped his driver on the ground.

"Nah, I work here," Crawford said. "I'm not a member."

"Oh, yeah?" Hardin said. "You own or rent your house?"

Crawford thought it was kind of an odd question.

"Rent at the moment," Crawford said, picturing his parking-lot view. "Why do you ask?"

Hardin slid his club into his bag and took a step toward Crawford, a big smile on his face.

"'Cause I'm a real-estate agent."

Balfour chuckled as Hardin came a step closer to Crawford.

"Just got a nice new listing down on South Ocean last night." Hardin touched his chin thoughtfully and started nodding. "Yeah, might be perfect for you. Actually has its own putting green. Plus a pool and a tennis court. You know, the works."

Crawford glanced over at Balfour who looked amused.

"I got a feeling it might be a little out of my price range." Crawford said.

Balfour guffawed.

But Hardin didn't notice. "Or I got another one in the Estate section. Recently renovated Mediterranean, really great bones. Only six million nine."

Crawford held up his hand. "Earl, I hate to break it to you, but I'm a cop." He said. "And, unfortunately, not a cop with a trust fund."

It was like Hardin just got drilled in the nuts with a golf ball. His eyeballs actually seemed to pop. "What?" he said, as if Crawford had just confessed to being a Charles Manson disciple. "What do you mean, a cop?"

"Well, actually a detective," Crawford said. "We make a couple bucks more than sanitation workers, but their hours are a lot better. So, unfortunately, that Mediterranean with the really great bones, not 'til I get a *really* big raise."

Balfour burst out laughing. "Earl normally plays with CEOs and hedge-fund guys, not a guy who handcuffs people for a living."

Crawford laughed. "I got a rich second cousin," he said, smiling at Balfour. "Maybe he could step up to the plate."

But by then, Hardin had lost all interest and walked back to his spot on the range. Crawford was dead to him.

"Hey, detective," the voice behind Crawford said.

He swung around and saw Sam Pratt, the man he had interviewed two days before.

"Hey, Mr. Pratt," Crawford said. "How's it going?"

"Sam," Pratt said, shaking Crawford's hand. "I'm guessing we're in the same foursome--" flicking his head at Balfour. "Numbnuts here said he had a special guest. Guess he meant you."

"I don't know, maybe meant Earl over there," Crawford said, turning to Balfour.

"No, I meant you," Balfour said. "This crowd could use some new blood. I've heard all his lame stories--"glancing at Pratt, then to Hardin-- "and all about his renovated Mediterraneans with really good bones.'"

Pratt smiled and Hardin scowled.

"So you got anything on Knight Mulcahy yet, Charlie?" Pratt asked.

Crawford shook his head. "I can't really get into it," he said. "I'm sure you can understand."

"Charlie was the one who put away Ward Jaynes last year," Balfour said, snapping off a 4-iron shot.

Ward Jaynes was a billionaire who had a thing for young girls. Turned out to be a killer, too.

"Good work," Said Pratt, pulling out his Taylor M3 driver. "That guy was a real a-hole."

"Not to mention murderer," Balfour said.

Pratt nodded. "Well, yeah, there's that."

Balfour looked at his watch. "All right, boys, we're up in ten minutes," then turning to Crawford. "You probably want to hit a few more balls 'stead of shootin' the shit with these bozos."

\*\*\*

him."

"I'll get over it," Ott said. "Anybody else he go off on?"

"At one point he launched into the Royal & Alien Club."

Ott laughed and nodded. "Bet he had a field day with that."

Crawford's cell phone vibrated in his pocket. He pulled it out, looked at the number and punched it.

"Crawford."

"Charlie, we got a homicide at 120 Middle Road." It was a woman named Barbara in Dispatch. "Where y'at?"

"In the building," Crawford said, standing up and flicking on speakerphone. "What else you know?"

"Body's in a car in the garage. Shot multiple times. House is owned by a man named Jabbah Al-Jabbah."

Ott stood up and grabbed his jacket.

"Thanks," Crawford said. "We're on our way."

\*\*\*

Jabbah Al-Jabbah's garage was not like most garages. It was the size of half a polo field, accommodated fifty cars, and not a drop of oil or a speck of dirt was anywhere to be seen. All there was were rows of vintage Ferraris, Lamborghinis, Maseratis in one section, and in another, American muscle cars--Pontiac GTOs, Plymouth Road Runners, Ford Mustangs, and two 1949 Oldsmobile Rocket 88s in moss green and candy-apple red.

Two uniform cops were on either side of a black Ferrari. It had a front windshield that looked like ten guys had unloaded their clips into it. Twenty feet away another uniform was talking to a tall, skinny man in his fifties with a dark complexion. As Crawford approached the Ferrari he noticed the passenger side window was blown out and saw broken glass on the gleaming white floor of the garage.

Crawford nodded at the two guys standing next to the car, one of whom was taking pictures with his cell phone. Then Crawford looked inside the Ferrari. A man who appeared to be in his twenties, though it was hard to tell since he didn't have much of a face left, was slumped down, his hands still on the Ferrari steering wheel. The leather seat was covered with blood and glass.

Crawford looked up at the uniform. "What do you know, Art?"

"Went down about forty, forty-five minutes ago," Art Nystrom said, flicking his head. "Man over there owns this place and is uncle of the vic. Heard what he described as the sound of firecrackers, grabbed a gun and ran down here. Saw a white car--didn't know what make it was--go haul-assing outta here right behind a vintage Ferrari Testarossa."

"So motive was car theft?" Crawford asked.

"Apparently," Nystrom said. "But not just any car; thing was worth over two million."

Crawford nodded.

"What's the vic's name?" Ott asked.

"Amir Al-Jabbah," Nystrom said, then flicking his head toward the tall, skinny man. "He's that guy's nephew. Jabbah Al-Jabbah is his name."

Crawford looked around the garage, then pointed. "We got a bunch of security cameras."

Nystrom nodded. "Yeah, but the hitter sprayed 'em. At least the ones we checked so far."

Ott turned to Crawford. "So the hitters were boosting the Testarossa," he said. "Then the nephew showed up?"

Crawford nodded. "I guess, but it looks more like an ambush. Like the hitters were waiting for the vic." He turned to Nystrom. "Art, go check around the house. See if there are any cameras that didn't get sprayed. Maybe we'll get a shot of the Ferrari, who was in it. White car too."

Nystrom nodded and he and the other uniform walked toward the oversized open door of the garage.

Crawford glanced over at the third uniform talking to the owner. Ronnie Riker had a pad out and was taking notes. Crawford walked over to them as Ott continued snapping pictures on his iPhone of the car and the dead man.

Riker nodded at Crawford as he walked up to them. "Hey, Charlie," then turning to the man next to him. "This is Mr. Al-Jabbah, the uncle of the deceased. This is Detective Crawford, homicide."

Al-Jabbah just nodded and made no move to shake hands.

"I'm sorry about your loss, Mr. Al-Jabbah," Crawford said.

"Thank you," Al-Jabbah said, his eyes unblinking and penetrating. "I do not want my nephew staying in the car any longer than necessary."

"I understand," Crawford said. "We'll try to make it as quick as possible. The Medical Examiner should be here shortly."

Crawford and the ME, Bob Hawes, had had a rancorous relationship on the three murders they had worked on together. Hawes thought Crawford was a cocky New Yorker; Crawford thought Hawes was a pig-headed redneck.

"He and the crime-scene techs need to do their investigations," Crawford explained to Al-Jabbah.

Al-Jabbah nodded. "I want you to make it fast."

Mort Ott came up to them.

"Mr. Al-Jabbah," Crawford said. "This is my partner, Mort Ott. Mr. Al-Jabbah is the uncle of—"

Ott nodded. "Sorry about your loss," he said.

Al-Jabbah nodded again, this time more impatiently.

"We need to ask you a few questions, if that's all right," Crawford said.

"Okay," Said Al-Jabbah, "go ahead."

Ott had his pad and pen out. He was the designated note-taker, since he had once complained--back when he and Crawford first started out--that there was no way in hell he could read Crawford's chicken-scratch notes. Told him his handwriting was worse than a doctor.

"Your nephew, how old was he?" Crawford asked, and he could see the past-tense jarred Al-Jabbah.

"Twenty two."

"And can you tell us about him?" Crawford said. "Did he work? Was he in college or what? As much information as you can provide, please."

"He is a student at Palm Beach Atlantic University and is staying here with me. He is my brother's oldest son. My brother lives in Saudi Arabia."

"And Mr. Al-Jabbah," Ott said, "this is a tough question, but do you have any idea if someone might have had a motive to kill your nephew?"

Al-Jabbah cocked his head and chuckled derisively. "Detective Ott, my nephew is a college student," he said. "Who in the name of God would want to kill him?"

Ott thought for a second. "Well, then, is it possible that whoever did it was targeting you? Mistook your nephew for you maybe."

The chuckle was more derisive. "That's absurd. No one wants to kill me either."

Crawford waded in. "So then, you think this was just a robbery? Your nephew just happened to drive in, in the middle of it?"

Al-Jabbah shrugged. "That's the only thing it could be. They took the most expensive car."

Crawford saw the ME walk through the wide front door of the garage fifty feet away.

"Here comes the Medical Examiner," he said. "Bob Hawes is his name."

Hawes went straight to the car and didn't even glance over at Crawford and the others.

Crawford thought for a second. "Mr. Al-Jabbah, I don't know much about cars like these," he gestured, "but aren't they kind of like expensive paintings? Someone steals one and it's pretty tough to sell. Because everyone knows it's been stolen and no one wants to touch it?"

Al-Jabbah thought for a second. "It is harder, but I'm sure there is a market for it in a foreign country. Somewhere in South America maybe. Why don't you do your job and check out boats? Ones leaving from Miami maybe."

Crawford nodded, having had his fill of Jabbah Al-Jabbah. "Thank you. We're going to go over and talk to the ME," Crawford said to Al-Jabbah as he pulled out his wallet and handed him a card. "Call me anytime. My partner and I will keep you in the loop on the investigation. If I could get your number, please?"

Al-Jabbah gave him his cell phone number, turned abruptly and walked toward a door to the main house.

"I don't know about that guy," Ott said, after Al-Jabbah walked away.

"What don't you know?" Crawford asked.

"I don't know."

Crawford smiled and looked over at Bob Hawes. "Come on, time to go talk to Mr. Personality."

## SEVENTEEN

Crawford called it "zig-zagging." Going from one homicide to the next. He'd much rather stay on one case from beginning to end, without the distractions of another one. But being one of two homicide cops in Palm Beach--Ott the other--that was not always possible.

Crawford had woken up at three in the morning, but the reality was that he had never really fallen asleep. Well, maybe ten minutes here, then wide awake, then fifteen minutes there, then wide awake again, then tossing and turning with snatches of sleep. He just kept thinking that maybe he and Ott were missing something about Knight Mulcahy's checkered life. As far as Amir Al-Jabbah went, it was just too early.

At 3:10 he got up to stay up. He tuned to iTunes and started going over re-runs of Knight Mulcahy's shows. He'd heard his show before, but more as back ground noise when he was in his car, his focus being on something else. There was a lot more bombast and bluster than he remembered. A lot of the time it seemed that Mulcahy was almost completely unfiltered, which now made sense, based on what Crawford had heard about him before his one month of sobriety. Going straight from his "Bloody lunches" right into the studio and immediately going on the air. In fact, the more he listened, the more certain segments seemed like nothing more than drunken rants.

At 5:30 a.m., Crawford got dressed and went to Dunkin' Donuts. Jeanelle served him his medium extra-dark and he took the coffee and two blueberry donuts back to his apartment. The donuts had a nice crusty crunch to them, which was just the way he liked them. The coffee was the way it always was--hot and good.

He clicked iTunes back on and listened to Mulcahy go off on Florida governor Rick Scott's misshapen, bald head along with, "his 75 IQ and serial-killer eyes."

At 8 a.m., he was still tuned in, thinking it was about time to hop in the shower and head to the station. He got up and walked to his bedroom. Just as he got to the door he heard Mulcahy say the words, "which was the same day I took my first walk on the wild side."

Crawford stopped dead, turned around, sat back down in his faux leather recliner with the twin cup holders and just listened.

"Hey, you gotta share the love in life," Mulcahy went on, seemingly by way of explaining his previous shocker. "Ravelasian guys like me gotta spread it around."

'What the hell was he talking about?' Crawford wondered, as he paused iTunes and popped open his MacAir and typed Ravelasian in Google. The first definition he got--once he figured out that it was actually *Rabelaisian*--was,"of, relating to, or resembling the work of Rabelais, esp. by broad, often bawdy humor and sharp satire." He checked out Rabelais in Wikipedia. The picture of him was a man with an unnaturally long head with a weird, four-sided, lumpy black hat perched on top of it.

None of that shed much light on Mulcahy's "walk on the wild side" comment, so Crawford Googled the line itself. Of course, the first thing that came up was the song by Lou Reed, which was, in fact, Crawford's source for what he thought the phrase meant. Crawford's take was that Mulcahy was coming clean--with clearly no remorse--about some kind of sexual act outside of normal male/female sexual congress. For many—most maybe—a 'walk on the wild side' meant a gay liaison, but, based on what he was learning about the life of Knight Mulcahy, it could have been anything from simple voyeurism to a romantic relationship with a neighborhood pet.

Crawford went back and hit the iTunes button. Mulcahy had now shifted out of the 'wild side' conversation to some political ramble that was only quasi-intelligible.

Crawford clicked off iTunes, went and got a jacket and tie and headed across the bridge to the station.

\*\*\*

He got in at 9:30 and went over to Ott's cubicle.

Ott looked up then made a big production of looking at his watch. "Meet a cute girl at Dunkin' Donuts or something, Charlie?"

Crawford's usual check-in was 8:00.

"Funny," Crawford said. "Gotta question for you: what does, 'walk on the wild side' mean to you, Mort?"

"Means you met a cute *guy* at Dunkin' Donuts."

Crawford ignored the comment. "So it means hooking up with someone you normally wouldn't hook up with, right?"

Ott chewed that over for a second. "Yeah, more or less," he said. "If your normal go-to is a woman, it would mean a guy or a transvestite or a--"

"Yeah, okay," Crawford said sitting down. "So I spent half the night listening to the best of Knight Mulcahy and at one point-- totally out of the blue—the guy says how one day he took a walk on the wild side."

"Really?"

Crawford nodded.

"That was it?" Ott asked. "No more details."

"No, it was pretty short," Crawford said, "like, I don't know, maybe that guy Skagg Magwood mighta been giving him the 'ol--" Crawford pantomimed a gesture of cutting his throat.

"Cut him off. Like he didn't want listeners knowing Knight had gone poofter?"

"Something like that."

Ott shifted in his chair and cupped his chin. "So what are you thinking?"

Crawford shrugged, remembering what Dominica had conjectured. "I don't know, that maybe it was a *guy* who had the little rendezvous with Mulcahy down at his pool house."

## EIGHTEEN

Crawford had gone back to his office. He made a call on his landline.

"Rose Clarke."

"Hey, Rose, it's Charlie."

"Hey, Charlie," Rose said. "This isn't your cell number."

"I'm at the station," Crawford said. "So I have kind of a strange question."

Rose laughed. "I like strange," she said. "Fire away."

Crawford exhaled, wondering just how to phrase the question. "So," he decided to start out broadly, "what have you heard about Knight Mulcahy's sex life?"

"I thought I told you," she said. "Prolific, in a word."

"And strictly heterosexual?"

"Funny you should ask," Rose said. "'Cause as macho as the guy was, there were these murmurings."

"About what?" He didn't want to lead the witness.

Rose sighed. "Okay, Charlie, you've gone past your allotment of free questions."

"Happy Hour at The Conch," he offered.

"You're not getting off that cheap," she said. "Lunch at Whitney's."

Crawford faux-sighed. "You got a deal."

"Okay," said Rose. "Now what's the question again?"

"About those murmurings you heard."

"Oh, yeah, that Knight was bi," Rose said. "Well, the way I heard it, he was maybe not...fully committed, more like a 'dabbler.'"

"A 'dabbler?'"

"Yeah, the occasional bromance."

The obvious question. "Like with who? You got names?"

"Okay, now it's gonna be dinner at Whitney's *and* a nooner."

Crawford laughed. "Come on, Rose, just a name or two."

"Well, I heard about this guy who was a riding instructor. Over in Wellington, I think," she said. "I don't know his name. Then another guy who's a waiter at Cafe L'Europe. Renny something. I've seen him and he's a real dreamboat."

Crawford was taking notes. "Anybody else?"

"Not that I can think of."

"This riding instructor, you know where he...rides?"

"In the back of Knight's Bentley maybe?"

"Naughty girl. The place where he *teaches* riding."

"I think it might be, Wellington Riding Academy," she said. "I can find out for sure."

"Yeah, please," he said. "So any other guys he 'dabbles' with?"

"I'll check my sources, but you *definitely* owe me a nooner."

"Rose, as tempting as that sounds, I got two murders."

Crawford heard a door shut in the background.

Rose lowered her voice. "I gotta go, Charlie, I'm at an Open House."

***

Crawford went back down to Ott's cubicle.

Ott was on the phone. "Email it to me, will ya?" He listened. "Yeah, 'preciate it."

He hung up and turned to Crawford. "Evidence tech is sending me the shots of the shoe impressions. Not sure they're gonna help."

"Well, at least we'll have the exact size," said Crawford. "So more on the theory of it being a guy down at the pool house."

Ott leaned forward eagerly. "Yeah?"

Crawford nodded. "Yeah, word is 'ol Knight may have had a

few toy boys parked around town."

# NINETEEN

Crawford and Ott were on the campus of Palm Beach Atlantic College, just across the bridge in West Palm Beach. It described itself as a faith-based, Christian college, which struck Crawford as a little weird since Amir Al-Jabbah certainly seemed about as Muslim as you could get.

What Ott had found out in a phone conversation with the dean of Students was that Amir was a 22-year-old Computer Science major, who had spent his junior and senior high school years at nearby St. Andrews School in Boca Raton. He was the son of a prince in the royal family of Saudi Arabia.

Ott had requested a meeting with the dean and asked him if it would be possible to see if some of Amir's classmates would attend. The dean seemed eager to cooperate and said he'd do whatever he could.

"What's this guy's name again?" Crawford asked as they walked into an administration building on South Flagler.

Ott pulled a piece of paper out of his breast pocket. "Ah, Dean Hoogesteger, I think you pronounce it. Easier if we just call him Dean."

They walked up to a receptionist and said the dean was expecting them. She led them into his office. Four people were there. The dean, behind a big mahogany desk, and three students.

"Gentlemen," said the dean standing and reaching across his desk to shake hands. "I'm Howard Hoogesteger--"then turning to the students--"and these three boys were friends--or at least knew–Amir. That's Josh"—he pointed to each one as he gave their names—"Logan and Sam."

They all shook hands and sat down in the extra chairs that the receptionist had brought in.

"Well, first of all, let me say to all of you," Crawford said, "we're sorry about what happened to Amir and will do everything

"That was totally bizarre," Ott said, as they waited for the drawbridge over the Intracoastal to go down.

"Which part?"

"All of it," Ott said. "Wonder what Uncle Jabbah thought of his nephew?"

"I doubt he knew the half of it."

Ott nodded. "I mean the bedroom with all the flags," he said. "Like Uncle Sam lived there or something."

"Yeah, it's weird," Crawford said. "But like you said, the whole thing was weird. The skinhead thing being the cherry on top."

"But the uncle, too," Ott said. "I mean, the car collection. Did he strike you as a guy who knows the difference between a '66 GTO and a 2016 Bentley?"

"What are you thinking?" Crawford asked.

"Almost like he was trying to show how American he is."

Crawford nodded. "Yeah, I hear ya."

As they rolled up to the station, Crawford turned to Ott. "I'm gonna go talk to the riding instructor in Wellington."

"You found out his name?"

"Yeah, my source left it on voicemail," Crawford said.

"Your source, as in Rose," Ott said.

"One of the definitions of a source, you don't disclose their identity."

"Even to me?"

"Especially to you," Crawford said. "Why don't you go to Cafe L'Europe. Check out the waiter there. "

Ott nodded as he opened the car door. "Gotta make a few calls, then I will."

Crawford watched Ott walk toward the station and hit the accelerator.

\*\*\*

Twenty minutes later he was in Wellington, a town in Florida you'd probably most likely go to if you were an equestrian or a polo player.

Jamie Delgatto was the name of the riding instructor. Crawford had tracked him down with help from Rose Clarke and set up the interview to take place at his stable at the Wellington Riding Academy.

Crawford had no idea how pungent a stable could be until he walked into it. He saw a man and a woman talking at the far end as he walked past a snorting chestnut-colored horse with a white patch between his eyes. He remembered riding a horse—just once in his entire life—and how he felt that it was an experience he never needed to repeat again. He never did feel in control. Plus it hurt his crotch. And that smell….

The man, wearing tight beige pants and a red jacket, turned to him. "Detective Crawford?"

"Yeah, hi," said Crawford, putting out his hand. "Mr. Delgatto?"

Delgatto shook his hand. "Yes," he said. "And this is Fredrika Bloomquist."

"Hi," Fredrika said. "Detective, huh?"

"Yes," Crawford said. "Palm Beach Police Department."

"I see," she said.

Fredrika Bloomquist was unclassically beautiful--eyes too close, nose too big--but somehow it all worked. Quite nicely, in fact. Incredible cheekbones, big, seductive lips, and long, flowing, dark brown hair.

"Well," she said, turning back to Jamie after taking in Crawford. "I'm gonna run. Have a nice ride, detective--"then glancing down at his khaki pants and loafers--"doesn't look like the most comfortable riding outfit."

"Thanks," Crawford said. "But I'm staying on terra firma."

"Well, nice to meet you," she said then turning to Delgatto. "See you on Thursday, Jamie."

## TWENTY

Turned out--according to Ott--Renny, the waiter at Cafe L'Europe, was a size twelve. Furthermore, he had been a long way from Knight Mulcahy's party, down in Key West for the night with one of his restaurant's regulars.

Crawford went back to his office, took off his jacket, hung it on the hook behind his door and sat down in his chair.

He leaned back and thought about what he had. In two words, not much.

Two homicides and not one solid suspect for either one.

He had two interviews scheduled for later in the afternoon. The first one was with Tommy Sullivan, at whose house, according to Mike Dickerson, Sullivan and some friends watching a football game had come up with the odds on who killed Knight Mulcahy. He and Sullivan had played telephone tag for a while but finally had spoken and set a date. The second interview was with Jabbah Al-Jabbah, the uncle of Amir.

After a half an hour of follow-up and returning calls, Crawford stood up, got his jacket and headed to Tommy Sullivan's house.

Sullivan lived in a big Mediterranean up on Emerald--not that there was any such thing as a small Mediterranean anywhere in Palm Beach.

Sullivan answered the door wearing gray flannel slacks and a pressed long-sleeved blue shirt that looked hot for the 85-degree day.

"Come on in," Sullivan said, one hand around a Perrier bottle. "Sorry we kept missing each other."

"No problem," Crawford said, following him into a large living room that had bright colored upholstered furniture everywhere. "Thanks for seeing me."

"You're welcome," Sullivan said and he pointed to a comfortable looking club chair. Crawford sat down, then Sullivan sat down opposite him.

"So," Sullivan said. "I know why you're here. I'm not going to get in trouble for that pool of mine, am I? It was really just kind of a joke."

Crawford shook his head. "Nah, no law against it. I just wondered if you knew something, or heard anything that my partner and I are not aware of concerning the death of Knight Mulcahy?"

"Probably not. I mean, I seriously doubt any of the guys in our pool did it, except maybe one guy I just added to it."

Crawford's head jerked up. "Who's that?"

Sullivan lowered his voice, though it was hardly necessary. "This is definitely off the record, right?"

"Definitely."

"Guy named Algernon Poole. He's an English guy who's a butler for Harold and Nancy Miller," Sullivan said with a big grin. "You know what they say, right?

Crawford thought for a second. "Oh, you mean, *the butler did it?*"

"Exactly," Sullivan said, nodding enthusiastically and taking a sip of his Perrier.

"I didn't even know butlers were still around," Crawford said.

"In Palm Beach? Oh, you bet they are," Sullivan said. "A bunch of 'em. He's kind of this upper-crust guy. Born a baron, I heard."

Crawford shrugged. "So tell me why you think he might have done it."

"Harold Miller is in my regular golf foursome," Sullivan said. "He told me one time, just out of the blue, that ol' Algernon was banging—ah, having sex with—Jacqui Mulcahy."

"O-kay. So—"

"So Harold's theory is that Algernon may have seen a future in the relationship if Knight were…in the past." Sullivan smiled leather chair next to him.

Crawford sat down.

"I just wanted to talk to you a little more about your nephew," Crawford said. "We just don't think the people who killed him were there to steal your Ferrari."

"What do you think, then?" Al-Jabbah asked.

"A car like that is just too visible," Crawford said. "Yes, someone could drive it into the back of a truck and keep it off the highway, but–going with your theory about putting it on a boat bound for South America–customs is gonna catch something like that nine out of ten times."

"Okay, then what do you think their motive was?" Al-Jabbah asked.

"They were either there to kill Amir or you." Crawford said.

"Preposterous," Said Al-Jabbah. "I said this before. Who would want to kill a twenty-two year-old college kid? Or me? I do not have any enemies."

"My partner and I have looked into Amir," Crawford said. "And here's what we've found out. Probably a few things you'll find hard to believe. Like the fact that Amir was what I'd call an extreme nationalist. In fact, it seems, more American than most kids born in America. He had no tolerance for anyone who challenged the system. Like there was a Black Lives Matter protest on the Palm Beach Atlantic campus that he and some friends protested against. And speaking of his friends, do you know what skinheads are, Mr. Jabbah?"

Jabbah looked as though he just caught a whiff of some noxious odor that had just blown in from a sulfur factory.

"Those people with the swastikas and tattoos?"

"Exactly," Said Crawford. "Your nephew was involved with them."

"That's ridiculous," Jabbah said. "My nephew was a Muslim."

"Seems like he might have strayed off course a little."

"What is that supposed to mean?"

"It means that Amir briefly belonged to a group called Hitler Youth," Crawford said, "Then after that, another group called Rockwell Forever, named after a man named George Lincoln Rockwell, who started the American Nazi party a long time ago."

Jabbah's jaw had gone slack.

"The group Amir was in had eight members," Crawford went on, "but one of them told my partner and me that a core belief of theirs was the holocaust never happened."

Al-Jabbah emitted a sound that was somewhere between a sigh and a groan. "Amir and I weren't that close. I—I didn't know any of this," he said faintly.

"That's what we figured. And I'm sure Amir didn't want you to know about any of it," Crawford said. "But our thinking is, someone--maybe a target of Amir and his group-might have had a reason to kill him, as unlikely as it may sound. Another possibility, though I'd say it's a long shot, is someone in his group killed him. That's what happened to George Lincoln Rockwell; he got shot by a man who used to be a member of the American Nazi Party."

Al-Jabbah sighed and shook his head slowly.

"I know it's a lot to absorb," Crawford said.

Jabbah glanced slowly around the room, then back to him. "Try to find the people who did this."

***

Five minutes later Crawford was walking down the long hallway out of the Royal & Alien Club. Coming in the front entrance of the club were three men. One was a huge black man with white hair in tight ringlets--Crawford figured he was close to seven-feet tall--who looked vaguely familiar. Crawford was guessing an NBA player from twenty years ago. The second was a short Hispanic-looking man, and the third--wearing Raybans--was...*holy shit!* His boyhood idol, Juke Jackson!

Crawford head-to-toed Jackson as he approached him and was silently questioning the sartorial match of Juke's black lizard boots and resplendent crimson pants. It reminded him of the kind of outfit Bill Murray would throw together at the Pebble Beach golf tournament.

Crawford caught Jackson's eye when they were ten feet away from each other. Jackson gave him an easy smile and a nod, like somehow he knew that Crawford had every single one of his albums and had been to twelve of his concerts. "How ya doin', brother," Juke said, as they passed.

Juke Jackson had just made Crawford's day. Even with all he'd been through: sniffing horseshit, hearing about men dressed up as women and skinheads protesting Black Wives Matter rallies.

## TWENTY-ONE

"My idol, Juke Jackson," Crawford was saying in Ott's cubicle, "I mean, right up there with the Springs!"

"The Springs?" Ott said. "Who the hell are you talking about?"

"Come on, man, who ya think? Bruce Springsteen and Rick Springfield."

Ott's frown was instantaneous. "Rick Springfield, are you fucking kidding me? One-hit-wonder Rick Springfield...you're not tryin' to put him in the same category as Bruce?"

"No, but he's sure as hell's no one hit wonder." Rock n' roll was one of the few things that got Crawford this animated.

"'Jessie's Girl....' What else?" Ott asked.

"Right off the top of my head, 'Affair of the Heart,' 'Don't Talk to Strangers," Crawford said, "and if you give me time to think, I'll come up with five more."

A voice came over the transom from the cubicle next to Ott's. "Don't forget that album, 'Working Class Dog.' Thing was killer."

Crawford looked over the top of Ott's cubicle and saw the bald-head and mustached face of Arnie Wolfe, a burglary detective.

"Now there's a man with taste," Crawford said, giving Wolfe a five. "You believe numbnut's here calling Springfield a one-hit-wonder."

"The hell do you expect," Wolfe said. "He's from Cleveland. Home of Marilyn Manson and Weird Al Yankovic."

Ott jumped out of his chair and craned up over the cubicle at Wolfe. "Wrong on both counts, dipshit. Marilyn Manson is from Canton and Weird Al is from somewhere in California. Never set foot in Cleveland, far as I know. You're thinking of Frankie Yankovic, the king of polka."

Then from another cubicle. "What about the O'Jays and those lame-ass Nine Inch Nails?" It was Frank Devon, white-collar crime.

Ott swung around to Devon. "Got a problem with Nine Inch Nails, asswipe?" He said, heatedly. "What about the James Gang and Joe Walsh? Rock 'n roll gods! And, by the way, the O'Jays–again Canton, not Cleveland, for fuck's sake."

Suddenly Norm Rutledge, chief of police, appeared, shaking his head.

"What the hell's all this racket back here?" Rutledge said. "They can hear you in the next county."

Crawford smiled at Rutledge, something he rarely did. "Just a little music debate, Norm."

Rutledge shook his head and looked like a parent ready to put the cane to a misbehaving child. "Correct me if I'm wrong, Crawford, but don't you have two unsolved homicides?"

Crawford glanced over at Ott, who was rolling his eyes.

"As usual, Norm, you are absolutely right, we do have two unsolved homicides," Crawford said, looking around at the cubicle dwellers. "Music debate's over, boys. As usual, Ott's got his head up his ass."

Crawford's cell rang. He looked down at the number and clicked on.

"Hey, Rose," he said. "I'm in a meeting. Can I get back to you in a little while?"

"Okay," she said.

He clicked off.

"That's part of your problem, Crawford," Rutledge said, gesturing at Crawford's phone. "Spend too much time talking to women."

That was a new one.

"*Really?* Are you kidding me, Norm?" Crawford said, truly outraged. "That woman–just so happens–is way more valuable than any C.I. we've ever had. I mean, gimme a fuckin' break."

Crawford quietly seethed as he waited for Rutledge to go back to his office. Finally, Crawford heard his door close.

He looked down at Ott, who was back on his computer.

"Come on, Mort," he said, "let's get the hell outta here."

"Mookies?"

"Yeah," said Crawford, "best place I know to solve crimes and quench your thirst at the same time."

## Twenty-Two

Mookie's was rowdier than usual. A retirement party for a West Palm motorcycle cop. They had two beers apiece and went back to the station.

Crawford didn't expect to find Harold and Nancy Miller's phone listed. But it was.

He dialed and a woman with a French accent answered. "Miller residence."

"Yes, hi," said Crawford, "I'm trying to reach Algernon Poole, please."

"Algernon does not work here anymore, sir," the woman said. "He works for Mrs. Mulcahy. The widow of Knight Mulcahy."

Crawford did not see that one coming. "Okay, well, thank you very much."

Crawford hung up and walked out of his office to Ott's cubicle.

"So the butler I told you about--"

"Algernon Poole?"

"Yeah," Crawford said. "Guess who he's working for now?"

Ott stroked his chin. "Hmm, I'm gonna guess...the widow Mulcahy?"

"Bingo," Crawford said. "Despite your musical deficiencies, you're not so dumb after all."

Ott stood up and shook his head.

"Where ya goin'?" Crawford asked.

"With you. To Q & A this Algernon guy."

Crawford shook his head. "I gotta bigger job for you," he said. "There's something about Jabbah Al-Jabbah that's begging for an exhaustive Mort Ott research job."

"You flatter me 'cause you don't want to do it," Ott said.

"Just tellin' it like it is," Crawford said, "Somehow you're able to find out shit nobody else can."

Ott smiled. "It's all right there in the public record."

"All of it?"

"Well, almost all." Ott asked. "So what's your hunch about Al-Jabbah?"

"I don't know, can't say I really have one. Just something about the guy," Crawford said. "I mean, he doesn't strike me as one of those Middle Eastern guys you read about who has five wives, drops a million bucks shopping in London. Like that guy Dodo whatever–guy who bought it with Princess Di."

"Dodi."

"Yeah, him," Crawford said. "I just got a feeling you're gonna dig up something good."

"Are you coming back here after you see Poole?"

Crawford nodded. "Yeah, but I got one more stop after him. One of Amir's skinhead buddies."

*\*\*\**

A tall man opened the door at 1250 North Ocean Way and his expression didn't change as he looked out at Crawford. He reminded Crawford of the actor in an ancient movie called "The Night Porter." Crawford wasn't sure whether it was Laurence Harvey or Dirk Bogarde. He always got those two mixed up. He just remembered seeing Charlotte Rampling for the first time in the movie and having the hots for her. Still kind of did, even though she was probably in her sixties now.

"Mr. Poole?" he asked.

"Yes," Poole said, taken aback that this stranger knew his name.

"I'm Detective Crawford, Palm Beach Police Department, I'd like to talk to you," he said.

Crawford couldn't tell whether Poole looked scared, confused, or put upon.

"Talk about what, detective?"

Crawford was on a step, one foot lower down than Poole. He didn't like Poole being able to look down at him.

"It's gonna take a few minutes; is now a good time?" Crawford asked stepping up to the landing.

"Yes, now is fine," Poole said, "the lady of the house is out. Come in."

They stepped into the large foyer and Poole stopped, turned and faced Crawford.

"So what would you like to know, detective?"

Crawford stood as straight as he could but Poole still had two inches on him.

Crawford decided, screw it, he might as well dive right in. "Mr. Poole, are you, or were you, having an affair with Jacqui Mulcahy?"

Poole scowled and went into mock-shock. "Hah," he said. "You have got to be kidding me."

For the first time, Crawford noticed he had one of those protruding Adam's apples.

"It's a simple yes or no question."

"My answer is, of course not, I work for the lady," Poole said. "And the question is totally outrageous and offensive. Since when does the Palm Beach Police Department go around demanding to know about peoples' love lives?"

"Actually, I was asking about your sex life. But let's move on," Crawford said. "My understanding is that you were at this house the night Mulcahy was killed."

Poole shook his head and sighed, offended again. "I was here because I was acting as chauffeur for the people I worked for at the time. They were guests at the Mulcahy party." Poole gave him a look like he wanted to add, 'you stupid fuck,' but was too refined for that.

Crawford nodded. "And you stayed in the Miller's car the entire time that they were at the party?"

"The entire time," Poole said. "Well, except for getting out a few times to smoke a cigarette--"then, an afterthought—"and going to see if that poor man was okay."

"What poor man?" Crawford asked.

"You didn't hear about that," Poole said, shaking his head, "a man Knight Mulcahy threw down the steps?"

Crawford realized who he was talking about. "A man wearing a double-breasted blue blazer?"

Poole nodded. "Which was probably missing a few buttons after Mulcahy got done with him,"

"And was he all right?"

Poole sighed. "He was, but I've never seen anybody madder."

"What did he do?"

"He just got up and went to his car," Poole said. "I heard him yell something right before he slammed the door."

"What was that?"

Poole looked around like he didn't want Jacqui Mulcahy suddenly walking in. *"Eff-ing* asshole." He said it in such a way that it almost sounded like a complement.

"So then he drove off?"

"No," Poole said, "he didn't go anywhere for a few minutes. Then he got out of his car and walked round the house."

"To where?" Crawford asked.

Poole shrugged. "I don't know, I didn't follow him."

"Did he come back when you were still there?"

"Yes, about fifteen minutes later."

This was big news.

"What kind of cigarette do you smoke, Mr. Poole?" Crawford asked, remembering what Poole had said earlier.

"English Ovals, why do you ask?"

"Because there was a cigarette butt found close to where Mr. Mulcahy's body was found." Crawford made it up to see how

Poole would react.

"Well, I can assure you, it wasn't mine."

Crawford went into auto-nod and didn't say anything for a few seconds. His way of implying he had his doubts about what he was being told. He looked at his watch. He had to meet the skinhead in fifteen minutes.

"Okay, Mr. Poole, I appreciate your time," he said. "If you wouldn't mind, would you give me your cell-phone number, please?"

Poole gave him a look like indeed he did mind.

"In case I have further questions," Crawford said.

Poole gave it to him.

"Thank you," Crawford said. "English Ovals, you said."

Poole nodded.

"And your shoe size?"

"You must be joking."

Crawford shook his head.

"Nine and a half," Poole said.

Crawford turned, walked out the front door and down the steps.

Dirk Bogarde. Definitely.

***

Businessmen have expense accounts to take clients and associates out to five-star restaurants for Kobe steaks and fancy bottles of wine. Crawford had an expense account to take skinheads out to chow down on SuperSonic cheeseburgers and Barq's root beer.

Mengele Johnson talked with his mouth full. He talked a lot, too.

Mostly about Jews, "spics" and "schvartzes" until Crawford cut him off and said he didn't want to hear the guy's racist rants any more. Didn't want a guy with a swastika on his neck to think he could say any damn thing he pleased. Even in the land of the free, home of the brave.

But he was curious about one thing. "I'm guessing that Mengele is not the name you were born with?" *Or else your parents were every bit as fucked up as you appear to be.*

Johnson laughed. "Dwight was the name I was born with. After that old chrome-dome president Ike," he said. "I couldn't lose that fast enough. Wanted a name that had a lot of history behind it."

Crawford bit his lip and didn't say that though president Dwight D. Eisenhower didn't do much, what he did do was a damn sight better than what Nazi Joseph Mengele did.

He watched Johnson noisily finish off his cheeseburger. The man was like a horse at a trough.

"So, Mr. Johnson, you have any kind of theory who might have killed Amir Al-Jabbah?"

"Don't be so formal. Call me Mengele," Johnson said, wiping his mouth with the sleeve of his shirt. "See, what happened was, a former colleague of mine broke away from HY and started his own organization."

Crawford took out his notebook, started writing, then looked up. "HY as in Hitler Youth?" He was going to play it like he didn't already know about a lot of this just to see if Mengele's story was consistent.

"Yeah, exactly," Johnson said. "So Amir--misguided little fuck he was--decided he wanted to join up with this other group-"

"What's the name of that one?" Crawford asked.

"Rockwell Forever," said Johnson. "Named after the guy who started the American Nazi--"

"Yeah, okay, and what's the name of the guy who started it?"

"Lonnie Bates," Johnson said. "Lonnie likes cars. In fact, word is he used to run a chop shop before he went legit and started managing a body shop in Lake Worth."

Crawford sensed the conversation might bend around to

Jabbah Al-Jabbah's collection of million-dollar cars.

"Why are you volunteering all this, Mr. Johnson?"

"'Cause I'm not a big fan of Lonnie's," Johnson said. "Guy's a dirtbag."

Crawford nodded.

"So anyway, Lonnie came up with an initiation for Amir," Johnson said. "To steal one of his uncle's cars and donate it to him."

Crawford stopped writing and looked up at Johnson who had just shoveled a ketchup-splattered fistful of French fries into his mouth.

"But it wasn't like Lonnie could drive it around," Crawford said. "Every cop in south Florida would be looking for it–" then something clicked–"you're not saying he was going to chop it for parts?"

"Nah," Johnson said, ketchup smeared all over his upper lip, "that would have been a total waste. Can you imagine chopping a Ferrari Testarossa for its parts? No, Lonnie occasionally peddles coke and has a buncha connections in Colombia–"

"So, you're saying he was going to sell it to some rich South American?" Crawford said, thinking maybe Jabbah Al-Jabbah's theory had some merit after all.

Johnson was nodding. "Specifically, some drug lord down there," he said. "You know, the Colombian equivalent of El Chapo or somebody."

"So is that what happened?"

"No. Way I heard it, Amir started thinking about it and figured he'd be in deep shit if he ever pissed off his uncle," Johnson said. "You know, kill the golden goose. Plus his uncle is, s'posedly, a dude you *really, really* do not want to go sideways on."

"Why do you say that?" Crawford asked. "What's the word on him?"

"I never met the dude," Johnson said. "But story is just don't fuck with Uncle Jabbo."

Which was Crawford's sense, too. "So Amir killed the idea of stealing one of his uncle's cars, then what happened?"

Johnson noisily slurped the rest of his root beer, then looked up. "Well, this is just Mengele coming up with theories, right?"

"Yeah, go on."

Johnson had ketchup on his lower lip and root-beer foam on his upper. He was hard to look at but Crawford forced himself to anyway.

"So Lonnie gets into the uncle's garage 'cause Amir told him how, then he just waits around 'til Amir shows up—"

"Yeah?"

"Then he pops Amir and steals the Ferrari."

"But why'd he pop Amir?" Crawford asked.

"'Cause he figured if Amir's alive you guys might put the pressure on him. You know, do what you do, stick him in a little room, act like you're his buddy, get him a Coke, then get him to spill his guts."

Crawford had to hand it to Johnson—that was pretty much the drill.

Mengele shrugged. "If Amir's not around, there's no way to finger Lonnie. Simple as that."

"Know where I can find Lonnie?"

"Like I said, he manages a body shop over in Lake Worth," Mengele said. "On Route 1 just before you get to 10th Street. Right side."

Crawford nodded and thanked Mengele.

It was a theory, and it certainly could have happened that way, but he wasn't yet sold.

\*\*\*

Ott was clearly excited when he saw Crawford come into the bullpen area and walk toward his office.

"Charlie–" he said, waving Crawford over.

Crawford stopped and walked into Ott's cubicle. "Got something, bro?"

"Bet your ass I do," Ott said. "Sit down and listen up."

Apparently, Ott had spent the morning logging onto some obscure web sites only he seemed to know about. Crawford knew this because he'd had trouble in the past getting Ott to divulge their names. Almost like they were his own personal snitches. Looking at his notes every so often, Ott told Crawford what he had found out about Jabbah Al- Jabbah. To start with, Jabbah was fifty-eight years old and was born in Riyadh, Saudi Arabia.

"Know who else was born in Riyadh, Saudi Arabia, and would have been fifty eight years old today?" Ott asked.

Crawford shrugged.

"Here's your clue," Ott said. "He'd be fifty eight if he wasn't killed five years ago."

Crawford thought for a second. "Bin Laden?"

Ott smiled, nodded and kept going. Turned out that Bin Laden's family had close business and social ties to Al-Jabbah's family and they both went to the same elite secular equivalent of high school. Bin Laden from 1968 to 1976 and Al-Jabbah from 1970 to 1976.

Then, Ott said, they went their separate ways and there was no trace of any communication or contact between the two until 1997. At that point, the CIA discovered that Al-Jabbah--living in Florida–sent a $20,000 check to Mullah Mohammad Omar, allegedly in support of a madrassah associated with him.

Crawford asked him what a madrassah was and Ott explained that it was a school where boys and young men got Muslim religious training.

Mullah Omar was an ally of Bin Laden, and it was suspected, though never proven, that the money from Al-Jabbah helped finance the bombing of U.S. embassies in two East African cities, Dar es Salaam and Nairobi. Additionally, it was thought that some of that money might have gone toward the intended sinking of a

U.S. destroyer in Yemen by an explosive-filled skiff that rammed into it.

Ott delivered the information matter-of-factly but authoritatively.

"Good job, man," Crawford said, when Ott was done. "You did that like some C.I.A. black-op bad-ass delivering a briefing."

"Why, thanks, Charlie," Ott said. "But I got a lot more digging to do."

"I'd say it's time we have another conversation with Al-Jabbah," Crawford said.

"And while we're at it, have one with his ex-wife too," Ott said.

Crawford cocked his head. "Didn't know about her," he said.

"Yeah, lives in a big condo on the ocean."

"Got a number?"

Ott nodded and gave him Fadiyah Al-Jabbah's number. Then Crawford told him about what Mengele Johnson had told him about Al-Jabbah: how he was a man even a sinister neo-Nazi didn't want to fuck with. After that, he proceeded to fill in Ott on what Algernon Poole had told him about the man in the double-breasted blue blazer, whose name, depending on who you listened to was either Bob or John.

At the end of Crawford's monologue, Ott put his feet up on his desk and leaned back. "Well, old buddy, I'd say we have two serious persons of interest."

# Twenty-Three

Bill was considered the best waiter at Marbella in Boca Raton. By far. He was forty one, tall--six-three or so--and had wavy hair that women always complimented him on. He was also entirely reliable--his boss could never remember him taking a sick day--and Bill made the dinner specials at Marbella sound like they were going to be the best meals you'd ever eat. He had an actor's cadence in his delivery and diners hung on his every perfectly-articulated word. Bill also had the stamina of an iron-man competitor and routinely did lunch and dinner shifts on his feet from twelve noon until ten o'clock at night, with a little breather in between from two thirty to four. During that time he read books. The writers Tom Wolfe and J.D. Salinger seemed to be two of his favorites.

The manager of Marbella, Don Clingerman, was a huge fan of Bill's because there was no doubt in his mind that he contributed directly to the restaurant's bottom line. Clingerman knew that because when patrons called up to make lunch or dinner reservations they would often ask to be seated at a table where Bill was the waiter. That was particularly true of single women and especially older ones. Clingerman had, in fact, heard it through the grapevine that Bill had been seen out on dates with certain older single women patrons. A movie here, an out-of-town restaurant there. But Bill appeared to be very discreet and his actions on the side never got in the way of his being a wait-staff rock star.

Unlike what Clingerman suspected--that Bill was having sex with some of the older women patrons--Bill had, in fact, a strict no-sex policy. Or maybe it was that he just didn't have much of a libido. In any case, he was--to use an old-fashioned phrase—strictly a "walker." Meaning he took money from them for essentially being an escort. And he also never crossed the line and went out with married women. In addition to non-sexual gigolo duty, Bill had a quite active social life, but one that he wasn't keen on people knowing about.

Another iron-clad rule Bill had was never to talk about himself. To the contrary, he prided himself on being an accomplished listener. He had a standard line: 'I know all about myself, and it's a pretty dull story, so tell me about you.' And whoever it was that he was with would be off and running.

One time, though, he violated that rule. Normally, he was a moderate drinker–two drinks then he'd switch over to water. But a year and a half ago he had made an exception. And lived to regret it.

It was his fortieth birthday and he felt like whooping it up a little. What the hell, he figured, he was somewhere around the halfway mark and might as well celebrate it. He had ordered a bottle of champagne and not just any champagne, but Dom Perignon 1990. He paid dearly for it, too, even though he got a discount because he was, after all, Bill-the-best-waiter-in-Boca-Raton. The bubbly got him talking and damned if he and his date for the night, Maureen–whose last name he had long since forgotten--didn't end up having two bottles.

They were talking about where each of them was originally from, since native-born Floridians were something of a rarity.

"So when you say 'up north,'" Maureen said, "that's a big area; where specifically?"

"A little town in New Hampshire you've never heard of."

Maureen perked up. "I went to summer camp in New Hampshire--where?"

"Place called Jaffrey, more cows than people."

He actually had grown up in Bennington, Vermont.

"I've heard of it, southern part of the state, right?"

Bill smiled, nodded then finished off what was left in his champagne glass.

They were at a place called Oscars in West Palm Beach, twenty-five miles up the road from Boca Raton. Bill had silently critiqued their waiter and found him wanting in several categories: One, he brought them Perrier when Bill asked specifically for Pellegrino.

Two, he stacked their plates when he cleared the table. And three, the most egregious sin, he referred to notes when telling them what the specials were. That was *so* bush league.

They were off in a corner, just dark enough for Bill's liking, and it had gotten late–there were just two tables of diners left.

"So keep going," Maureen said, "tell me what it was like growing up in quaint little Jaffrey?"

"Boring and way too much snow," Bill said. "I couldn't wait to get out of there."

"So you went through high school there?" Maureen asked.

"No, actually, I went away to school," he said, almost apologetically, "a boarding school."

"Oh," Maureen said, clearly more than a little surprised, "a rich kid."

Bill chuckled. "Well, for a while anyway."

"What do you mean?" Maureen asked, taking a dainty sip of her Dom.

"What happened was, my parents took me out after my junior year," Bill said, refilling his glass. "My father had... what you would call, a business reversal or two."

"I'm sorry to hear that," Maureen said, then another dainty sip.

"Yeah, well, it happens," Bill refilled Maureen's glass.

"What was the name of the school?" Maureen asked.

"It was called St. Paul's, up in Kan-kud."

"Kan-kud?"

"That's how New Hampshire people pronounce it," Bill said. "It's actually Concord, capital of the Granite State, in fact."

He really had gone to a boarding school, but one called Choate.

Then Maureen asked him a few more questions and Bill told her about his father's furniture manufacturing company going under because China came along and started making stuff for half of what United States companies could make it for. He told her about going back to high school in Jaffrey and not really fitting in. How there was no money to send Bill and his sister to the kind of colleges they were expecting to go to. About going to Rindge Community College and flunking out because all he did was sit around and drink Schlitz beer all day long.

Substitute Bennington for Jaffrey and Community College of Vermont in Montpelier for Rindge CC and it was all true.

***

What he didn't tell her, and never would tell anyone, even if he had five more bottles of Dom '90, was about the incident. The thing that had happened in 1985 that caused him to hastily pack up his Plymouth Valiant in the middle of the night and simply drive, with no destination in mind. The thing that had gotten him to change his name and never speak to his parents or sister again.

He realized he didn't have much more to say to Maureen, nor she to him. He figured it was about time to pack it in, get his $200 from her and give her a quick, passionless good-night kiss.

"Well, looks like they're about to give us the ol' last-call-for-alcohol," he said. "By the way, I love that dress."

Bill was also an all-star flatterer.

Maureen looked down at the flowery number she had on. "Oh, thanks," she said. "It's a Lilly."

"I figured," said Bill.

She must have felt that she should return the compliment. "Last time you wore that same jacket. I have to say, Bill, there's nothing more sexy than a man in a double-breasted blue blazer."

## TWENTY-FOUR

Crawford called Jabbah Al-Jabbah and asked to meet with him later in the day. Jabbah was irritated and asked what hadn't they covered in their first two meetings. Crawford said he just needed a clarification or two and Jabbah said, "Well, ask me right now and I'll clarify." Crawford said he preferred his interviews be in person and, after a long dramatic sigh, Al-Jabbah said he had a golf game that afternoon but would meet him–briefly–after that. They agreed to meet at the Royal & Alien at five.

In the meantime, Ott would dig around some more and see what else he could find out about Jabbah.

At 4:40, Crawford swung by Ott's cubicle. Ott was on his computer and his printer seemed to be spewing out page after page, based on its overflowing tray.

Ott was so tuned in to what he was reading on his computer that he didn't hear Crawford approach.

"Got something good there, fat boy?" Crawford asked.

"You wouldn't believe this shit," Ott said, not looking up. "How 'bout a tie-in between Jabbah Al-Jabbah and one of the 9/11 guys."

"You're kidding," Crawford said, hunching down to read what was on Ott's screen.

"Be easier if I just summarize it for you," Ott said, grabbing the pages out of his printer tray.

When Jabbah Al-Jabbah first moved to America, Ott explained, he had ended up in Sarasota, Florida, after having been a principal in a firm in the United Arab Emirates that helped multinational companies establish businesses in the Middle East. He also was a cousin of Khalid A. Nasser, CEO of Aramco, the trillion-dollar Saudi Arabian oil company. Jabbah's next door neighbors in Phoenicia, a prestigious gated-community in Sarasota, was the Ghazani family. Two days before 9/11, the Ghazani family--all nine members--suddenly disappeared from their house in the middle of the night. They left half their possessions there and never returned. Six weeks after 9/11, based on a tip that twenty one year old Abdul Ghazani was taking flying lessons at Huffman Aviation in Venice, where several of the 9/11 pilots had learned to fly, FBI agents stepped in and investigated.

What they found, on the Phoenicia's digital automobile scan system, were atleast two license plates registered to Mohammad Atta and Ziad Jarrah, two 9/11 terrorists. The two had, allegedly, visited the Ghazani house several times in the month leading up to the attacks. Atta had piloted one of the planes that flew into the World Trade Center and Jarrah had crashed landed near Shanksville, Pennsylvania. The men had purportedly identified themselves to Phoenicia security guards by their real names when they first drove in.

"You're gonna ask if I found any definitive connection between the 9/11 guys and Al-Jabbah. Well, the answer is no, but, I mean, it's way too coincidental that two families from Saudi Arabia just happen to end up next-door neighbors."

Crawford nodded. "Yeah, and Atta and Jarrah spent time at the neighbor's house," he said. "It would be nice if we could come up with a direct link between Al-Jabbah and them. I mean, like Al-Jabbah paying for their flying lessons or something."

"Yeah, but if the FBI didn't, I wouldn't be real optimistic we're gonna," Ott said, putting the pages down on his desk.

"Which brings up another point," Crawford said. "We've got to assume that Jabbah is on the FBI watch list because of this and the Mullah Omar and Bin Laden connection."

"I know," said Ott. "And with all their resources, they must either think he's clean or they don't have enough on him."

Crawford looked at his watch. "Well, we're gonna be face-to-face with the man in fifteen minutes," he said. "Guess we'll see what he's got to say."

***

Crawford finally figured out who Jabbah Al-Jabbah reminded

him of. A guy who he'd seen on ESPN playing Texas Hold 'em on the cable TV show, "World Series of Poker." The guy was Chinese or Korean and Crawford couldn't remember his name, but for a solid hour, or however long the show lasted, his expression never changed. Impassive was the word for it. Whether he had just made or lost two-hundred thousand on a hand, his expression always stayed the same. It turned into a joke, the other players trying to make him smile or frown...something...anything. But his expression never changed. Then, about a year later, Crawford tuned into another poker show and there he was again. Long hair and a wispy mustache now, but the same flat expression.

***

Crawford and Al-Jabbah were sitting in the same room and in the same chairs at the Royal & Alien as they had been in last time. Except now it was a triangle, with Ott facing both Al-Jabbah and Crawford. On the ride over Crawford and Ott had agreed to initially go back to the premise that Amir Al-Jabbah had been shot during the commission of a car robbery in Al-Jabbah's garage then see where it went from there.

"That's exactly what I told you," Jabbah responded, "when we were in the garage right after Amir was killed."

"I know you did," Crawford said, "and now we have a possible suspect."

"Who?" Jabbah asked.

"A man named Lonnie Bates," Crawford said, looking closely to see if Al-Jabbah reacted to the name.

Just like the veteran poker player, he didn't.

"Who is he?" Jabbah asked.

Crawford glanced away, then his eyes came back to Al-Jabbah. "You remember last time I told you about a group called Rockwell Forever that Amir was a member of?"

Al-Jabbah nodded.

"Well, as part of his initiation to join the group," Crawford said, "this man, Lonnie Bates, might have tried to get Amir to steal one of a your cars."

Al-Jabbah remained impassive.

Crawford snuck Ott a look like it was now time for Ott to throw Al-Jabbah his high, hard curve ball.

Ott leaned forward in his chair. "Mr. Al-Jabbah," Ott started slowly. "On a different note, did you ever contribute money to the Taliban? Specifically, to a man named Mullah Omar."

Suddenly Al-Jabbah demonstrated that he had at least one more expression: outrage.

"What in God's name are you talking about?" Jabbah said, glaring at Ott.

"I was doing some investigating," Ott said, "and it came to my attention that, many years ago, you gave twenty thousand dollars to Mullah Omar in Afghanistan. Is that the case, Mr. Al-Jabbah? I also believe that Mullah Omar and Osama bin Laden were allies."

"This is totally outrageous," Al-Jabbah said. "Outrageous. As part of my philanthropic efforts, I may have once made a contribution to a madrassah in Afghanistan."

"Run by Mullah Omar?" Ott asked.

"I have no idea. He may have had something to do with setting it up a long, long time ago," Jabbah said.

"He did," Ott said. "Your contribution, was it made before or after Mullah Omar called for the extinction of all Americans?"

It had just become apparent that Al-Jabbah had a third expression Crawford had never seen before: pure, unadulterated hatred.

"Did you come here to my club to insult me?" he asked. "I thought you were public servants, men who taxpayers like me pay to solve crimes. Not men who go around hurling insults at people."

Ott had never had one ounce of back-down in him. "Mr. Al-Jabbah, I assure you we did not come here to insult you but to get information so we can catch your nephew's killer."

"Then why don't you go find this Lonnie character?"

Crawford's turn. "We have gone to where he works and where

he lives several times. He was at neither place. Don't worry, though, we'll find him."

"On another subject, Mr. Al-Jabbah," Ott was rolling now, and Al-Jabbah's frown indicated he might not be ready for another subject.

"In 1991," Ott said, "you moved to Sarasota from Saudi Arabia after living in the United Arab Emirates, correct?"

"Yes, so what?"

"There was a family named Ghazani who lived next door to you--" Al-Jabbah's frown intensified, "--did you know them?"

"Yes, I knew them. I'll ask you again, what does this have to do with the death of my nephew?"

"Did you also know Mohammad Atta and Ziad Jarrah, Mr. Al-Jabbah?" Ott asked.

Al-Jabbah sprang out of his chair. "That's enough of your insulting questions," he said. "You're supposed to be finding the killer of my nephew, not investigating me. I've been in America for twenty-five years paying taxes and minding my own business. Now get the hell out of here"--he raised his arm and pointed to the door-- "get out of here right now. And don't ever call me again."

Crawford and Ott got up, walked out of the room, down the hall, and out the front door.

Crawford turned to Ott once they were both inside the Crown Vic. "Two things," he said, "one, most people are going to know the name Mohammad Atta but not Ziad Jarrah."

Ott nodded. "Yeah, I don't remember ever hearing that name back when 9/11 went down."

"But Al-Jabbah sure as hell knew who he was," Crawford said turning on the engine.

Ott nodded. "And number two?"

Crawford put the car in gear and hit the accelerator. "Number two, we're definitely gonna hear about this little Q & A. 'Cause I guarantee you, Al-Jabbah's gonna raise hell and try to hang us out to dry. Rutledge's usually the guy who gets that job."

"Yeah," Ott rolled his eyes and nodded. "One of the few jobs he really likes."

# Twenty-Five

Fadiyah Al-Jabbah looked like a doe you'd come across in the woods. Wide-eyed and hyper, like If you moved a muscle she would race off at break-neck speed and never look back. She lived in a vast condominium, dominated by sixteen-foot ceilings and the best views of the ocean Crawford had ever seen.

Crawford felt the situation called for more warm-up chitchat than usual. So he had commented on the view and the houses beautiful decorating to the point where he thought he might be overdoing it.

Finally he had steered the conversation around to her relationship with her former husband and, right out of the gate, she had come up with a shocker: Amir Al-Jabbah had come to America to stay with his uncle two years after the death of their daughter, Lydia, and a year after Fadiyah divorced Al- Jabbar.

Daughter?

There had never been any mention or any sign of a daughter. But then, Crawford realized, he and Ott had never asked Al-Jabbah about his family, except for Amir. Fadiyah got up and went over and got a framed picture off of a piano and showed it to him. She was tall and gawky, but had a nice, shy smile. Fadiyah said she was a very bright girl, but very sensitive and always kept to herself.

Then Fadiyah put the picture down on a side table and asked Crawford if she could get him anything to drink. He said, no thanks, and she excused herself and walked out of the room. A few minutes later she reappeared with a wineglass filled to within a half inch of the top. He suspected she might have some unburdening to do.

Did she ever.

She explained how one time the burglar alarm went off accidentally in the Al-Jabbah garage and three squad cars from the police department showed up. That was the beginning of a friendship between her husband and members of the police department. They had stuck around that day to admire his cars and were particularly interested in the American "muscle" cars. That was a big surprise to Crawford, based on the cold reception he, Ott and the others had gotten when they arrived right after Amir's murder.

She explained how it became a regular thing that a few of the cops would come over to see his cars. They'd open the hoods and study the engines for hours. After a while, Al-Jabbah became comfortable enough to let them drive the cars. He explained to Fadiyah the cars were like horses, they needed exercising from time to time. One time he let several of them drive his cars in a Fourth of July parade.

Then one summer day, Fadiyah continued, her daughter Lydia had driven into the garage when two off-duty cops were with Jabbah Al-Jabbah studying the engine of a black Roadrunner. Al-Jabbar introduced her daughter to them and that was the start of a relationship between Lydia and Danny Burgess, an OCVAN cop, which stood for Organized Crime/Vice and Narcotics Unit.

"He was a very nice man, extremely polite, and took her to art exhibits and things at the Kravis," Fadiyah said. "We were happy for Lydia because she really hadn't ever had a beau before. It went on for quite a while and they seemed pretty serious."

Crawford was trying to place Danny Burgess but was pretty certain there was no one by that name in the Palm Beach Police Department.

"Only thing Danny forgot to tell Lydia was, he was married. We never found out about this until… after."

Crawford almost didn't want to ask her: after what? But he did.

"What happened, Mrs. Al-Jabbah?"

A single tear rolled down Fadiyah Al-Jabbah's check.

"Lydia never said a word to us," she got up from her chair. "Will you excuse me for a second?"

"Sure," Crawford said as she walked quickly toward the kitchen.

She came back in a few moments later with several Kleenex tissues and dabbed at her eyes with one. "Sorry," she said. "Lydia had a close friend, Janna, who she confided everything to. Janna told me afterwards that Danny promised Lydia he was going to leave his wife and marry Lydia. Not the first man to not deliver on that promise, I suppose. Janna told us that she suspected Danny was after Lydia's money."

Fadiyah finished off the last of her wine. "But then—very abruptly—Danny broke it off. The next night Lydia went to his house with a gun of Jabbah's and shot him four times. After that—" and the tears were flowing now—"she turned the gun on herself. They both died instantly."

Crawford wanted to touch her and comfort her but didn't think it was appropriate. "I am so sorry, Mrs. Al-Jabbah," he said. "I had no idea."

She nodded. He could tell she had more unburdening to do. "Something like that happens—the loss of a child—can either make a relationship stronger or..."

Crawford knew it was time to go.

But Fadiyah was not done.

"Several of the policemen came to the house to offer their condolences shortly after it happened—"she wiped her eyes with a Kleenex—"my husband went and got a rifle and threatened to kill them. They calmed him down, but that was the end of that relationship, too."

# TWENTY-SIX

It was 7:15 that night. Crawford and Ott were slouched down across from each in Crawford's office. Crawford had just told Ott the story about the death of Lydia Al-Jabbah. Ott said it now made sense why Al-Jabbah wasn't showing them the love.

They had the white board positioned on the wall behind Crawford that first had the names of the Mulcahy murder suspects and a timeline for them on the night of the murder. At the bottom of the whiteboard it said: 'Amir Al-Jabbah,' which was underlined, and below it, just one line, 'Lonnie Bates?'

They had no idea where Bates was at the time of Amir Al-Jabbah's murder because they had no idea where Lonnie Bates was. They had gone to where he lived and worked four times and had not found him. Now they had under covers posted around the clock at his house and the body shop he managed. His house was actually a double-wide trailer and the body shop looked—based to a large extent on the clientele--like it might do a side business in dealing drugs of some kind. On Crawford's second visit to the double-wide, Bates' girlfriend had told him that Lonnie had a habit of disappearing for a few days at a time and employees at the body shop made comments like, 'he'll probably be back shortly' or 'he'll be here in a little while.'

It had been more than shortly and much more than a little while and no Lonnie.

They were going down their list of Knight Mulcahy suspects one by one again, feeling like they had spent enough time questioning and investigating them all and it was now time for arresting, handcuffing and incarcerating one of them. Problem was, they were still a long way from having a suspect with a literal or figurative smoking gun in hand.

They had pretty much eliminated Jacqui and Paul Mulcahy, there was just nothing there. Same with Skagg Magwood, Lila Moline and Brewster Collett. They had checked them out further

Mort--figured maybe she took a shot or two that might be useful to you guys."

Crawford looked over at a nodding Ott. "Yeah, definitely can't hurt," he said.

"Thanks Rose," said Ott. "Might be very helpful. Who's the photographer?"

"Got a pen?" Rose asked.

"Fire away," Crawford said, figuring the more photos the better.

"Her name is Fredrika... Fredrika Bloomquist. and she's not really your type, Charlie. Or else I'd never give you her name."

## Twenty-Seven

Juke Jackson couldn't tell his daughter Jonquil that her mother used to be a groupie. But maybe, she'd already figured it out. Just had never brought it up. Because, among others things, her mother was the inspiration of at least three of the great rock n' roll anthems of all time.

Fact of the matter was Maggie Blacksmith was right up there with Pamela Des Barres, Bebe Buell, and Tawny Kitaen in the hierarchy of all-time, world-class, rock n' roll groupies.

Jonquil was one of those compromise names. Maggie--back when Jonquil was born in 1991--was going through a New Age phase and wanted to name her daughter Tranquil. But Juke, more of a traditionalist, wanted to name her after his mother, Joni. So Jonquil it became. It was only later that they discovered that was also the name of a flower, so that was an added bonus.

Jonquil was twenty-five now and made for a beautiful bride indeed as proud papa Juke walked her down the aisle of St. Edwards Catholic church on County Road.

Now the wedding party, three hundred strong, was at the reception being held at the Royal & Alien. It was a somewhat odd mix of people since the bridegroom was from Greenwich, Connecticut, and his preppy-looking parents and their friends looked as though they were no strangers to the world of polo, squash and debutante parties. The wedding party and guests were in two large rooms at the R & A--the main bar room and one that was called--'the Library.'

The Library, as the name indicated, had three walls of books from floor to ceiling. Sharonda White and Rachel Gold of the R & A Decorating Committee had found a place where you could buy books by the pound--five pounds for a dollar, to be exact. Two whole shelves of books were in German and there were at least two full Encyclopedia Britannica sets but it didn't matter because most of the R & A members were not big readers anyway.

On the third wall of the Library were landscape watercolors and lithographs, which seemed suitably club-like, with the exception of two oil paintings that hung side by side. One was of the soul singer, James Brown, who seemed to be wailing a song as rivulets of sweat poured off his brow. Another was of the comedian, Henny Youngman, with a microphone in his hand and a bad hair-do on his head.

The other room--called the Main Bar--was left over from when the club was called the Mid-Island Club. In fact, the Decorating Committee had decided not to touch it at all. It had lots of chintz and mahogany furniture and on its far wall and on the right wall was what everyone came for--one of the best-stocked bars in Palm Beach (currently, manned by three men in white jackets and black bow ties).

Juke Jackson was on the far left of the bar chatting up Marion Prendergast, who was Geoff the bridegroom's mother.

"That was really nice of your ex-wife to give the bridesmaids' luncheon yesterday," said Marion, who had been pounding flutes of champagne.

Juke laughed. "Actually, just for the record, Maggie never was my wife," he said. "But she loves doing stuff like that."

"She told me you two met at a concert where you were playing," Marion said, polishing off another flute.

"True," Juke said. "We were the warm-up act for the Stones in Denver."

"The Rolling Stones? As in Mick Jagger and that other one... the drug addict?" She said, slurring the last part so it came out, 'druck attic.'

"Yeah, good old Keith," Juke said. "Met Maggie then, a year later, we were the headliner there."

Juke could see Marion wasn't tracking. Not that it mattered.

It looked like her mind had wandered off to something else. Then she gave him a hard-to-decipher smile and a tilt of the head.

"So is it really true what Maggie told me about you?" Marion asked.

Uh-oh, thought Juke, this could go in a whole lot of strange directions.

"I don't know," he said. "What did she say?"

"About--"her fake eyelashes flapped like a hummingbird's wings-- "about all those phallaxes?"

"Ah, sorry, Marion, I'm not with you."

"You know."

"Honest, I don't," he said. "Phallaxes?"

Then suddenly it hit him. *Oh, Jesus.* "She told you about that? What exactly did she say?"

He immediately regretted asking the question. Because he knew ol' three-sheets-to-the-wind Marion was going to answer it.

"Well," Marion said, raising a finger to the bartender for a reload. "She said... let me make sure I got this right... she said"– giggle, giggle--"she said she made plaster casts of--how did she put it"--another giggle-- "oh yes, plaster casts of the *members* of the *members* of different bands. In other words, their penises--erect penises, that is--"

Juke put a hand up as if he was stopping traffic. "I got it, Marion," Juke said, thinking, *Hey, I was there, honey.*

Then he flashed to what a guy in another band told him, about how Maggie had like fifty of the damn things down in her basement. From Jimmy Hendrix to Frank Zappa to, supposedly three quarters of Kiss–not to mention, a roadie named Bart.

Marion was grinning and Juke was feeling like he'd rather be fishing in Idaho.

He saw Jonquil in her flowing white dress coming toward them, a big smile on her face. Saved by the bride!

She walked up and kissed Juke. "So glad you two are getting to know each other," she said, then kissed Marion on her over-rouged cheek.

"We were just talking about how beautiful you looked coming

"Oh, yeah, like what?" Crawford said, popping the last of the blueberry donut into his mouth.

"Well, like Habitat for Humanity, for one."

"No kidding, so you actually pound nails and stuff?"

"Pound nails, screw screws, you name it."

"Ever do any sheetrocking?"

Fredrika laughed and her thick mane of dark brown hair shook.

"No, but you're looking at a really good spackler."

"I'm impressed," Crawford said. "So what else?"

Fredrika thought for a second. "Well, I work down at the dog pound."

Crawford, in mid-sip, put his coffee cup down. "You do?"

Fredrika nodded.

"I keep toying with the idea of getting a mutt," Crawford said.

Fredrika laughed. "It's gotta be a mutt?"

"Yeah, well, when I was a kid, we always had mutts. And I loved 'em all --"then he remembered--"except this one named Bugsy. Ate our cat and took a chunk out of my brother's leg."

Fredrika was trying hard to suppress a laugh. "Really? Ate your cat?"

"Well, pretty close. All but her fake-diamond studded collar," Crawford said, launching into his second donut. "Poor ol' Pandora."

"Well, all our dogs are sweethearts, not one cat-eater in the bunch," Fredrika said. "Particularly the mutts."

"I really am thinking about getting one," Crawford said, washing down the donut with a long sip of coffee. "Problem is, I'd have to move."

"Why?"

"I'm in a condo now. No backyard," he said. "But a helluva view."

"Oh, yeah, of what?"

"The Publix parking lot."

Fredrika laughed. "Well, you just let me know when you're ready to come down to the pound," she said. "You'll get pick of the litter."

"Thanks," Crawford said, suddenly regretting getting Fredrika there under false pretenses. "I have a confession to make."

Her head reared back a little. "A confession?"

"Yes," he said. "Here's the thing, a mutual friend of ours said you were at Knight Mulcahy's party when he got killed and you took a bunch of pictures."

She nodded slowly. "And being a detective you'd like to see them, is that it, Charlie?"

Crawford nodded.

"Well, you could have just asked." She said. "I would have brought them with me."

"I should have," he said, leaning back in his chair. "Would it be too much to ask, if I followed you back to your house and took a look at them after here?"

Fredrika pulled her chair back and stood up. "Come on, let's go," she said. "Who is our mutual friend anyway?"

"Rose Clarke," Crawford said, standing up.

Fredrika turned back to him and winked. "Good ol' Rosie."

***

By Palm Beach standards, Fredrika lived in a small house. It was only around 3,000 square feet, Crawford guessed, but had a spectacular garden in back and beyond it a show-stopping view of the Intracoastal. She also had an art collection that--something told him--was worth a small fortune.

They were sitting on a couch in her living room looking at a stack of black and white photos.

Crawford had just commented on how professional the photos appeared.

"I was actually a freelance photographer up in New York," Fredrika said.

"No kidding. I was a cop up in New York for fifteen years," he said. "But we probably traveled in quite different circles."

Fredrika chucked. "Where'd you live?"

"Upper West Side," he said. "Upper, upper, upper—"he pointed at the photos—"These are really good, by the way. Nice composition. Kind of artsy. Like I have a clue what I'm talking about."

"Well, thank you, Charlie, that's nice of you to say," Fredrika said, then standing up. "Anyway, look through them. Maybe you'll see a murder clue somewhere in there. Sure I can't get you something to drink?"

"No, thanks, I'm fine," Crawford said, looking at the next photo. It was of a smiling couple in the foreground, the man had his arm around the voluptuous brunette.

Crawford was about to go on to the next when he saw in the background one of the men he had played golf with at the Poinciana a few days before. It was Earl Hardin—snob, bigot and golfer, who gave himself a gimme from anywhere inside of ten feet. He was going out one of the French doors in the back of the living room.

Crawford pulled the photo closer.

"Found something?" Fredrika asked coming back from the kitchen with a bottle of water.

"Probably not," Crawford said. "Just wondered if you knew who this was."

He handed her the photo. "The guy going out the back door."

Fredrika took a look.

"Oh, that's Earl Hardin," she said, like she might say, *Oh, that's Adolf Hitler.*

"Not your fave," Crawford said.

"Not really," Fredrika said. "But none of that Bush Island

crowd is."

Bush Island was twenty-five miles north of Palm Beach.

"Why? What do you mean?" He asked.

"I don't know, all those people from the land of pink and green are just so damned pleased with themselves."

"But isn't there a fair amount of that right here in Palm Beach?" He asked. "I mean the pink and green crowd."

"Well, yeah, I guess," Fredrika said, twisting a strand of her thick hair, "it's just different somehow."

Crawford nodded and went on to the next photo, hoping to see another shot of Hardin. But that was the only one and there weren't any others that piqued his interest.

He looked up at Fredrika. "Thank you very much," he said. "You really are a hell of a photographer."

"Thanks," she said. "I'm guessing you didn't spot your murderer in there?"

"Probably not," Crawford said. "So I'm dying of curiosity, anybody ever call you Freddie?"

Fredrika laughed. "My father. He's the only one I couldn't say, 'don't call me that,' to."

"Are you kidding? I think it's such a cool name," he said.

"I can't stand it." She looked him straight in the eyes. "So we had coffee, maybe we do a drink next? Even though you did lure me to Dunkin' Donuts under false pretenses."

"Absolutely," Crawford said. "Just as soon as things slow down for me."

"Do I detect a subtle blow-off?"

Crawford shook his head. "No, just a guy who's busy as hell at the moment," he said. "Can I borrow that one picture? Promise I won't lose it."

Fredrika smiled. "Sure. It's all yours."

Crawford stood up. "Thanks."

She took a step toward him. He could tell she was vectoring in for a cheek kiss.

He took a step toward her.

Instead, she gave him a quick kiss on the lips, followed by a smile. "So just let me know when it's time for that drink."

"I will."

## TWENTY-NINE

Ott stuck his head into Crawford's office.

"I been doin' some more diggin'," Ott said.

"As only you can," Crawford said. "And what did you come up with?"

Ott walked in and sat down opposite Crawford. "This time… Algernon Poole. Know what HOLMES is?"

Crawford shrugged. "A real-estate magazine?"

"No, spelled H-O-L-M-E-S."

"Like Sherlock?"

"Yeah exactly," Ott said. "Stands for Home Office Large Major Enquiry System. It's the Scotland Yard computer system that's got data on just about every crime ever committed over there."

"Keep goin'."

"So I thought I'd check out Poole, see if he's got any skeletons in his closet."

Crawford put his feet up on his desk. "What…was he the brains behind the Great Train Robbery or something?"

"How 'bout a suspect in a double homicide."

Crawford leaned closer to Ott. "You got my undivided attention, Mort."

"I'll email you the report," Said Ott. "But the gist is he worked in The City, which is London's equivalent of Wall Street, as a stock broker or something. What happened was this couple was killed, who turned out to be clients of his. Apparently he had some kind of fraud thing going where he'd siphon profits--pretty big money--from their account into a fictitious account, which he controlled. Scotland Yard guys found out about it after the couple was killed in what looked like a murder-suicide, but could never prove anything. Poole got convicted for the fraud racket and did a two-year bit, though. As soon as he got out, he came over here."

"No shit," Crawford said, sliding his feet off his desk. "Can you email me that?"

Ott stood up. "Sure, I'll go do it now." He said. "Oh, also got something on our writer friend."

"Durrell?"

Ott nodded. "Not as big as the Poole thing, but still pretty good."

"What did he do?"

"Bad case of road rage. Couple years ago up on Northlake Boulevard in Palm Beach Gardens," Ott said. "He cut off some kid and dragged him out of his car. He was on a bridge and threatened to throw the kid over the side. Got convicted for aggravated assault."

"Jesus Christ," Crawford said. "What's with these people? More goddamn loose cannons per square inch than any town in America."

"I don't know, man," Ott said. "Maybe something in the water."

Crawford just shook his head. "Hey, before you go, let me show you something."

Crawford slid the picture Fredrika had given him out of his breast pocket and handed it to Ott.

"Nice headlights," Ott said of the buxom girl in the foreground.

Crawford pointed at Hardin. "No, numbnuts, this guy. What's he look like to you?"

"Like a guy in a hurry to get somewhere fast."

Crawford nodded. "Not like a guy duckin' out to take a piss or sneak a butt?"

"Fuck no," Ott said. "Look at his eyes: he's a man on a mission."

By 3 PM the next day, Crawford had still not heard back from Earl Hardin whose number he had gotten from David Balfour. He had left four messages. Two on his cell and two at his office on Bush Island. He got the distinct impression that Hardin was ignoring him and that didn't sit well with him. He buzzed Ott and asked him to drop by his office.

A few moments later, Ott walked in. He was wearing what Crawford referred to as his "janitor at a funeral look." A maroon blazer, lightweight grey rayon pants, a white shirt, with his favorite brown and orange rep tie, white socks, and black, lace-up shoes.

"Lookin' natty today, Mort," Crawford said.

"Fuck off," Ott said, "sarcastic bastard you."

Crawford held up his hands, then explained the job he had in mind for Ott.

Ott dialed the number Crawford gave him.

"Mr. Hardin, please, Earl Hardin," Ott said to the woman who answered.

"Who's calling, please?" the woman said.

"A guy who wants to buy a house on South Ocean Boulevard," Ott said.

"Just a second, please," said the woman.

"Hello, this is Earl," Hardin answered, almost immediately.

"Hi, Mr. Hardin, my name is Mort Ott," Ott said. "I'm down here from Cleveland and I saw a house with your sign on it at 1108 South Ocean in Palm Beach. How much you want for that?"

"You're in luck, Mr. Ott, they just reduced the price," Hardin said. "It's only eleven point nine. Seven bedrooms, eight baths, a pool, and one of the finest wine cellars in Palm Beach."

"Oh, man, that's music to my ears," said Ott, "'cause I'm a big time oenophile. Got myself an award-winning collection of cabs and merlots. When can I see it?"

"How 'bout later this afternoon?" Hardin said. "I just need to drive down from Bush Island. Owners are out of town. Five o'clock work for you?"

"Perfect," Ott said. "See you then."

He clicked off and smiled at Crawford.

"Oenophile, huh," Crawford said, "is that like a pedophile?"

Ott chuckled. "Funny," he said. "Hey, I wonder if the guy'll think I'm natty enough to pay ten nine for his big ass crib."

"Thought it was eleven nine?"

Ott shook his head. "Come on, Charlie, you think I'm stupid enough to pay the full ask?"

***

An hour and a half later, Earl Hardin glanced over at Ott in the driveway of the $11.9 million house. His look said he doubted Ott could afford the mailbox.

Then Crawford got out of the Crown Vic, which was sorely in need of a wash, and Hardin's suspicion was confirmed.

He was seething.

He walked across the courtyard and up to Crawford. "You made me drive all the way down here for nothing?"

"We could go look at the house if that would make you feel better," Crawford said.

"Yeah," Ott said. "Wouldn't mind checkin' out that wine cellar."

Hardin didn't deign to even acknowledge Ott's existence. "What do you want?" Hardin asked, resplendent in a seersucker suit and bow tie with little bunny rabbits on it.

"Next time, call me back," Crawford said, his eyes cruising the exterior of the yellow Spanish-style house. "Eleven point nine seems a little on the high side."

"I said, what do you want?" Hardin repeated.

"Just a few simple questions," Crawford said as his eyes circled back to Hardin. "Where were you going when you went out the back door of Knight Mulcahy's house, the night he was murdered?"

Hardin didn't hesitate. "Home," he said. "It was a really boring party."

Crawford nodded. "You're married, right, Mr. Hardin?"

"Yeah. So?"

"Did your wife go with you?"

"We went there in separate cars," Hardin said, scratching his cheek. "She's always the last to leave."

"Mr. Hardin," Ott said, uncrossing his arms, "did you talk to Knight Mulcahy at all that night?"

"No, I barely know the guy," Hardin said. "Just there 'cause my wife knew his wife a little."

"But you both were members of the Poinciana Club," Crawford said.

"So? There are five hundred members," Hardin said. "I avoid his group. I don't know how they ever got in in the first place."

"So you never went down to Mulcahy's pool house?"

"Wouldn't even know where it was."

"Next to his pool."

"Well, yeah, no shit," Hardin said. "Told you, I went straight home."

"What did you do when you got home?" Crawford asked.

"Watched something on the tube."

"You remember what?"

"Something on the Golf Channel."

"You remember what?"

"Jesus, what difference does it make?"

"I'm trying to give you an alibi."

"For Chrissakes, like I need an alibi," Hardin said. "It was a replay of the Players."

Crawford glanced over at Ott who didn't seem to have any more questions.

Neither did Crawford. "Okay, Mr. Hardin," he said. "Thank you for your time."

Hardin slowly shook his head. "You're not welcome," he said. "I coulda sold a goddamn house in the time you wasted."

Hardin walked over to his car, opened the door, started the engine and gunned it. His Mercedes left a ten-foot strip of rubber on the white asphalt driveway.

Ott turned to Crawford and shook his head. "The Crown Vic could do better than that."

"Guy's not off my list," Crawford said. "What do you think?"

"A killer…umm, not so sure," Ott said, "An asshole? Hundred percent sure."

\*\*\*

On their way back to the station, Crawford's phone rang. He didn't recognize the number. He hit the green button.

"Hello?"

"Hey Charlie, it's Jerry Pournaras," said the undercover cop, "Lonnie Bates just showed up at the body shop."

"We'll be there in ten," Crawford said, hanging a hard right and flooring the Vic.

They actually made it in eight minutes. They drove up to Pournaras's Taurus parked behind a cluster of U-Haul trucks in a raggedy-ass lot across from the auto body.

Pournaras's window rolled down as they pulled up beside him. "Hey, boys," he said. "So Bates showed up in a green Charger, pulled into that second bay." He pointed at the auto body that had three bays.

"You made the plate?" Ott asked.

"Yeah, definitely his," Pournaras said.

"You see him get out?" Crawford asked.

"Nah, just saw two guys. Couldn't make 'em out."

Crawford turned the key and shut off the engine. "Come on, Mort, let's go have a chat with Lonnie."

They both got out of the Crown Vic.

"Need me?" Pournaras asked.

"Nah, we're good," Crawford said.

They walked across the street. It was seven-thirty at night but still around eighty-five in the shade.

Two sweating guys were under the hood of a red pick-up.

"We're closed," one said.

Crawford flashed them ID.

"Whaddaya want?" said the other, wiping his greasy hands on his overalls.

"Lonnie Bates," Crawford said.

"Hasn't been around in a few days," the first one said out of the side of his mouth.

"So that's not his car?" Ott said.

The first guy shrugged, like he hadn't seen it there before.

"Where is he?" Ott asked.

Both of them shrugged.

Crawford walked up to a closed door on the far side of the second bay.

'Where's this go?" Crawford asked.

"Nobody's there," said the second one.

"I didn't ask you that," Crawford said. "Where's it go?"

"Storage room," the second one said.

Crawford pushed open the door. There were no lights on. "Anybody in here, come on out," he said.

Nothing.

He walked in, Ott right behind him.

Crawford saw movement just before something hit him on the back of both shoulders. It was like the roof caved in on him, but, fortunately, missed his head. He slumped forward into a crouch but didn't go down all the way.

Then he saw another man with a five-foot two-by-four come down hard on Ott's shoulders. Ott fell forward with a loud groan.

As Crawford got to his feet the first man head-butted him in the ribs. Crawford didn't have time to think but slashed with his right hand hitting him in the back. Then again. Then a third time. The guy fell to the floor, head first. Crawford's shoulders felt like when a 300-pound linebacker speared him during a Dartmouth-Cornell football game.

The man on the ground beneath him started to move. Crawford kicked him in the left side. He stopped moving.

Jerry Pournaras ran into the dimly-lit room, his Glock drawn.

"Hands up, motherfucker," he said to the guy holding the two-by-four over Ott's head.

The guy dropped it and raised his hands.

Ott was on the floor, on all fours. "Fucking A," he groaned.

Crawford walked over to him, grabbed an arm and lifted him up.

Ott looked up to see who it was. "Fuckin' A, Charlie," he said. "Like a fuckin' head-on with a fuckin' semi."

Crawford had once counted five 'fucks' in one Ott sentence, so this was nothing. Crawford looked back down at the man on the floor he had beat on. He was moving now.

"Which one of you assholes is Lonnie Bates?" Crawford asked.

The guy standing looked down at the guy on the floor and flicked his head.

Crawford gave Lonnie Bates a tap with his shoe, then noticed Ott pointing at two square shapes the size of bricks wrapped in clear plastic and tape sitting on a wooden cable spool.

"Looks like coke to me," Crawford said to Ott.

Ott nodded and walked over to the round wooden spool. "Sure does," he said.

"We thought you were someone else," said the guy standing.

"What's your name, shithead?" Crawford said, raising his left arm gingerly to see if it was still working.

"Ronnie," the guy said. He was tall and skinny and had an old Mohawk that had grown out.

"Ronnie who?" Ott asked.

"Bates."

Ott shook his head. "Ronnie and Lonnie," Ott said. "Ain't that cute. Your parents, pretty fuckin' creative. Sister named Bonnie, by any chance?"

With great difficulty, Lonnie got to his feet.

Crawford looked at Pournaras. "Cuff 'em, Jerry."

"Hey, man," Lonnie said. "We thought you were tryin' to rip us off."

"So you sayin' we should just drop the aggravated assault charge, Lonnie? Pretend we didn't see the coke?" Crawford said, counting at least six tattoos on the man.

"What if we give you something you want?" Lonnie said.

"Like what?" Crawford said. "A lube job?"

Lonnie picked up his Harley Davidson baseball hat off the floor. "No, about what happened to Amir Al-Jabbah."

"Who?" Crawford played dumb.

"You know who," Lonnie said. "The kid who got killed at his uncle's garage."

"So what about him?" Crawford asked.

Lonnie pointed at the brick of coke on the wooden spool. "That goes away, right?"

Crawford looked over at Ott, then back at Lonnie and shook his head. "Depends on what you tell us."

"Come on, man," Lonnie said.

"Let's hear what you got," Crawford said. "May just be a buncha worthless shit."

Lonnie sighed. "Amir found out something his uncle was up to. Something his uncle didn't want him finding out about."

"And what was that?"

"I don't know," Lonnie said. "Amir never told me the whole thing."

Crawford shook his head. "Like I said, you might just have a buncha worthless shit."

"Kid said his uncle mighta had something to do with ISIS," Lonnie said. "Might be planning something."

Crawford looked over at Ott again. Ott wiped his mouth. "You use the word *might* a lot," Ott said. "Got anything that doesn't have might or maybe in it?"

"Said his uncle had these two converts he was training," Lonnie said.

"What kind of converts?" Crawford asked.

"To ISIS," Lonnie said.

"What else?" Ott asked.

"The uncle was pissed Amir found out." Lonnie said.

Crawford looked over at the less talkative brother. "What about you Ronnie? What do you got?"

"I wasn't in Rockwell," Ronnie drawled. "I just remember Amir sayin' he was scared shitless his uncle might do something to him. You know, 'cause he found out about the ISIS thing."

"What? The uncle thought Amir might tell someone?"

Ronnie nodded. "Yeah," he said, "about the converts, too."

"So bottom-line it: who you think killed Amir?" Crawford asked.

"I think the uncle coulda," said Lonnie. "Or gotten the converts to."

Crawford shook his head slowly. "Still hearin' too many 'shoulda's' and 'coulda's' and 'mights' and 'maybes,'" he said, then pointing at the coke. "How you figure that's making those bricks go away?"

## THIRTY-ONE

Crawford and Ott had just driven into the lot behind the station house, Ott was at the wheel. It was 7:15.

"We gotta call the FBI," Ott said.

"Yeah, but not 'til we got more," Crawford said.

"Why not now?"

"Like I told the lowlifes," Crawford said, "all we got is a bunch of suppositions. Plus they could fuck things up for us."

Ott nodded. "Yeah, it is the FBI."

Crawford's cell phone rang. He looked down at the number. It was Rose Clarke.

"Hey, Rose." He said as Ott turned off the Vic's engine. "I was actually just going to call you."

"Charlie," she was whispering, "I'm at a cocktail party and John, the man in the double-breasted blazer, is here. I thought you'd want to know."

Crawford reached across Ott's right leg and turned the ignition key back on. Ott gave him a confused look.

"Where are you?" Crawford asked Rose.

"114 Dunbar," she said. "Jimmy Pappas's place."

Crawford turned to Ott. "114 Dunbar," he said. "drive like you got a fire up your ass." Then into his cell phone. "Thanks, Rose, we'll be right there."

Five minutes later Ott pulled up behind a big red Mercedes on Dunbar Avenue. Cars were parked on both sides of the street. They got out of the Vic and hoofed it up to the front door of number 114.

Crawford tightened up his tie and wished his shoes were a little shinier as Ott pressed the doorbell.

A black woman in a black dress with white lapels opened the

door.

"Welcome," she said, "Mr. and Mrs. Pappas are out on the back patio with the other guests. Come right in."

"Thank you," Crawford said, noticing her eye Ott and his "janitor at a funeral" attire.

Then she turned and disappeared into the kitchen as Crawford and Ott walked through the living room and saw people out on the patio in back.

"Lotta pink and green out there," Ott observed.

"Team colors," said Crawford, opening the French door to the patio.

The patio was huge and looked out over a vast backyard with a tennis court at the far end.

Crawford scanned the crowd for the man in the double-breasted blue blazer. He saw a lot of men in blue blazers but not one double-breasted one. There were many people on the far side he couldn't see, though.

A tall man with curly white hair wearing lime green pants and a long-sleeved azure blue shirt walked up to them as they were taking in the guests. The man thrust out his right hand.

"Hey, fellas," he said, somewhat quizzically, "I'm Jimmy Pappas."

"Oh, hi," Crawford said as he saw Rose Clarke come up behind Pappas.

"Jimmy, these guys are friends of mine," Rose said, giving Crawford, then Ott a kiss on the cheek. "Hope it's okay I invited them over."

Pappas nodded enthusiastically. "Absolutely," he said. "The more the merrier. Bar's right over there."

Pappas slapped Ott on the back and walked away as Ott winced.

"You okay, Mort?" Rose asked.

"Yeah, I'm fine," he said. "Just some guy whacked me with a two-by-four a little while ago."

Rose looked over at Crawford. "He's joking right?"

Crawford smiled. "Yeah, you know jokin' Morty," Crawford said. "Where's our guy?"

"He's out there somewhere," Rose said looking out over the crowd of people on the patio. "I just had to duck into the bathroom for a second."

A young woman with a silver tray with a half dozen flutes of champagne came up to them.

"Champagne?" she asked.

"Ah, no thanks," Crawford said.

"Come on, you'll blend in better," Rose said. "One glass isn't going to cloud your brilliant detective mind."

"Don't mind if I do," said Ott, taking one. Then, under his breath: "For the pain."

"What the hell," Crawford said, taking one.

She smiled back and nodded.

"Let's circle around the other side," Crawford said. "Really gotta find this guy."

The three walked around the outer perimeter of the patio. Crawford saw his friend David Balfour chatting up a tall, wispy blond wearing aviators. Crawford recognized her from one of the pictures that the *Glossy* photographer had taken. He thought she was the woman with Paul Mulcahy.

"You know her?" Crawford asked Rose. "The girl with David Balfour."

Rose laughed and lowered her voice. "You mean the high-class call girl?"

"Come on," Crawford said. "*Really?*"

"Got news for you, your friend David's not above that," Rose said. "I think her name is Willow or one of those made-up kind of names."

Crawford turned to Ott. "She was the one with Paul Mulcahy

at his father's party, I think."

"No shit," said Ott.

"That makes sense," Rose said, lowering her voice. "Word is, Paul did some pimping for his father. Or acted as his beard sometimes."

"What's that?" Ott asked.

"You know, where you make it seem like a girl's with you," Rose said. "But really you're just a deliveryman."

"Isn't that interesting," Crawford said.

Ott started nodding. "You mean, she might have been delivered to the pool house?"

Crawford nodded back as he spotted a short man in a robin's-egg blue, double-breasted blazer and white ducks. "Not that guy?" he said.

Rose looked over and laughed. "No, that's Paul Whitman, owns that horse that won the Preakness."

"Where is he, Rose?" Crawford said impatiently.

"He was here fifteen minutes ago is all I can tell you," Rose said.

"Maybe left when you went to the bathroom?"

"Maybe."

"Shit," Crawford said under his breath.

"Sorry, Charlie, I thought I was helping."

Crawford exhaled slowly. "You were, Rose, I appreciate it."

He led her away from the crowd. Ott followed. "Rose, on another subject, Earl Hardin, broker up on Bush Island—"she rolled her eyes—"what's his reputation in the real estate business?"

"He makes a lot of money," Rose said. "Gets a lot of listings because he makes certain, let's call 'em, side deals."

"What do you mean 'side deals?'" Crawford asked.

"A lot of people who want to move to Bush Island have all the money in the world, but no connections," Rose said. "Meaning they don't know people in the club. And if you want to get into the club, you need someone to propose you, second you and write letters saying what a huge asset you'd be. Earl can make that happen...if, of course, you buy a house from him."

"So it's kind of a—"

"--quid pro quo," Rose said, nodding. "It also works the other way."

"What other way?" Crawford asked.

"Well, let's just say you're a guy from Queens who just struck it rich in the garment business and somehow you heard about Bush Island. Figure it sounds like a nice place to have a second home—" Crawford nodded as Ott moved closer to Rose—"You call up Earl's real estate company and Earl hears your accent and asks a couple of questions. Then he goes, 'Sorry, Mr... Whoever, but there's nothing available at the moment.' And Mr. Whoever says, 'What do you mean, I saw that place listed for twenty million on the Intracoastal and another one for sixteen million on the ocean,' and Earl goes--" Rose finished off her wine—"'Sorry, the one on the Intracoastal has a deed restriction that it can only sell to a club member and the one on the ocean is about to go pending.' Earl keeps goin' like this–putting up road blocks–and poor old Mr. Whoever gets sick of the runaround and finally figures fuck it, who needs it, I'll find a place somewhere else."

Both Crawford and Ott were shaking their heads.

"Wait I got more," Rose said. "Jesus, don't get me started on the guy. So, and this is more in the conjecture department, but I've heard it enough times to believe it's true. Earl has a real knack with little, old, rich ladies. They trust him 'cause... well, 'cause he's a pretty slick act. So they think he's going to take care of them, you know, do the right thing. So they call him up and say they want him to list their house. He rubs his hands together, slaps on his smarmy smile, and proceeds to get the listing. But what he does is get them to list it at a below market price--"

"What do you mean? How's that work?" Ott asked.

"Okay, so let's say, the comps say a house is worth ten million. Earl doesn't tell the sweet, little, old lady that. Instead he tells her it's worth *eight*. Then he goes to his buddy, Johnny Boyd, the contractor, and gets him to buy it for eight. I know that happened at least twice last year. So Johnny puts a million into it and sells it for fourteen million. Earl gets a six percent commission on the eight million sale, then another six per cent on the fourteen million dollar sale and, I suspect, Johnny gives him a piece of what he makes off of the flip for throwing the deal his way."

"Wow, I'm doing some quick math," Ott said, "that sleazeball probably made over a million bucks on that one deal alone."

"Yup," Rose said. "You do that a couple times a year and, guess what, it pays for one of the biggest summer houses on Martha's Vineyard, not to mention his shiny, new helicopter."

Crawford was silent, then finally, looking at Ott, said. "I could say something like, 'hey, we're in the wrong business, Mort,' but I'm just gonna say…a house on Martha's Vineyard, a shiny, new chopper, guy's still a lowlife sleaze bucket."

Crawford heard steps right behind him. "I thought that was you," a voice said.

Crawford turned.

Fredrika Bloomquist was wearing a short beige skirt and a sleeveless silk top with more than a suggestion of cleavage.

"Oh, hey, Fredrika," Crawford said.

"Hi, Charlie," Fredrika said, kissing him on the cheek, then to Rose, "Hey, Rose."

"Hi, Fredrika," Rose said with an impish smile. "Looks like you and Charlie hit it off."

Crawford wasn't going within five miles of that. "And this is my partner, Mort Ott."

"Hi, Mort," Fredrika said. "Nice to meet you."

"Back atcha," Ott said, like he was saying hello to a cop at Mookie's.

Crawford searched the crowd again for the man in the double-breasted blue blazer.

"Fredrika," Crawford said, "I hate to be rude, but we're trying to locate someone. We need to look around a little."

Fredrika held up her hands. "I understand. Do what you have to," then to Ott, "well, nice to have met you, Mort."

"Likewise," said Ott.

Crawford walked to the far corner of the patio, Ott and Rose right behind him.

Rose scoured the crowd, then shook her head. "I guess that's what happened," she said.

"You mean he left while you were in the can?" Ott asked.

Rose laughed. "'Fraid so."

Crawford turned to Ott. "Know that car that was leaving when we got here?"

"That black BMW?"

Crawford nodded. "Could have been him. He was headed toward Lake Way. Maybe a security cam caught him."

Ott nodded.

Crawford turned to Rose. "A big favor: If we find this car in the camera footage and can make out the driver, will you swing by the station and ID him?"

"Sure," said Rose. "No problem."

"Thanks," Crawford said.

Ott looked down at his empty champagne flute, then up at Crawford. "Well, Charlie, guy's not here, might as well have some more bubbly."

\*\*\*

A half hour later, Ott was holding court.

Fredrika Bloomquist, David Balfour, Leelee Pappas, Rose Clarke, and Crawford were listening to a story Ott was telling. Crawford wasn't listening too attentively because he had been there when it happened.

"So they were sittin' around skinny-dipping in their in-door pool when all of a sudden three alligators splash down into it--"

"Wait, what?" Leelee Pappas's jaw dropped a full inch.

"Yeah, I remember," David Balfour said, nodding. "Came through the air-conditioning ducts, right?"

Ott nodded. "Yeah, these Russian guys built the house with big commercial-sized ducts, so the guys who did it--posing as AC repair men--brought in the gators in a van and shoved 'em in on the ground floor."

"Killed the brothers and one of the women, right?" Rose asked.

Ott nodded. "Yeah, another woman who was there escaped."

"That's incredible," Fredrika said. "I didn't know alligators were aggressive like that?"

"They are when they're hopped up," Ott said.

"What do you mean?" Fredrika asked.

Crawford decided to throw in his two cents worth. "They shot 'em up with something called apostolyn. Same effect steroids have on bodybuilders."

"So you mean like 'roid rage?" Balfour asked.

"Something like that," said Crawford.

"Jesus," said Balfour.

Crawford turned to Ott. "We gotta get goin', Mort," he said, then to the others, "town doesn't pay us to hang around knocking back cocktails, tellin' war stories."

Ott looked disappointed. Like he was just getting started. "One more."

Crawford shook his head. "Let's go," he said.

Ott nodded.

Crawford turned to Rose and Fredrika who were standing next to each other. "Ladies," he said. "Nice to see you again. Wish we could stick around, but...."

"Bye, Charlie," said Rose, then turning to Ott. "See you, Mort."

Ott smiled and nodded.

"I'm going to call you in a little while about something else," Crawford said to Rose.

Rose smiled and nodded.

"Hope you catch the bad guys," Fredrika said, giving Crawford a long look then a short smile.

"Thanks," Crawford said, then he turned to go.

He and Ott walked through the house, down the front steps and out to their car.

Ott opened the driver's side door, got in and glanced over at Crawford. "First cocktail party I even went to, Charlie."

"Seriously?"

"Yeah, didn't have many up in Cleveland."

"C'mon, man, they have 'em everywhere," Crawford said. "You just didn't travel in the right circles. Until now, that is." He motioned with his hand. "Let's go see if we can find a tape of our mystery man."

## THIRTY-TWO

Jacqui Mulcahy and Algernon Poole were having sex on her ultra-king sized bed, which measured nine feet by nine feet. Jacqui was on top and Algernon was grunting like a mover who was lifting a heavy couch into a truck. As their lovemaking reached its crescendo, Algernon started slapping Jacqui hard on her buttocks. Then, even harder. At first she seemed to like it, but then it was just plain painful.

"Stop, that's too hard," she said.

"I thought you liked it rough," Algernon said, slapping her again. "That's what I heard through the grapevine anyway. You and Brewster Collett going at it with riding crops. So the story goes anyway."

Jacqui rolled off him and looked him square in the eyes. "What is wrong with you, for God's sake?"

"What do you mean, love?" Poole said. "Pain and pleasure, a very thin line."

"I'm talking about what you said," Jacqui said. "About Brewster Collett."

"Well, I hope it wasn't true," Poole said. "I mean, riding crops, please, that is *such* a cliché. Surely you could have come up with something more original than that. I overheard my former employer getting quite a chuckle out of that."

Jacqui sat up on the two pillows behind her and reached for the glass of water on the bedside table. "Just let me remind you, Algernon, you work for me. Don't blow it; you have a very good thing going here."

Algernon reached up, grabbed her arm and pulled her across his body in one swift motion. Then he smacked her three times— harder than before—on her buttocks.

"Ow," she cried out in pain, "stop that, goddamnit! What the hell do you think you're doing?"

Then she tried to wriggle free but he had her pinned.

He spanked her again on the buttocks three more times. This time you could see his finger marks on her.

"I'm going to tell you what the rules are around here, milady," Poole said, his mouth just above her ear. "One, you are prohibited from further assignations with Collett at the Breakers or anywhere else. Two, you will ask for my permission to leave the house, and three--" Poole took her arm and twisted it roughly up behind her back—"and three, you will do everything I tell you to do, because if you don't, you will end up like a certain former client of mine in London. I suggest you Google her. Her name is... *was* Lizette LeGrande--" Poole wrenched her arm up even farther—"may she rest in peace."

\*\*\*

Crawford was dialing David Balfour when Ott walked into his office. Crawford motioned for him to have a seat. Balfour answered on the first ring.

"Hey, David," he said. "That woman you were with last night at the Pappas party, I'd like to talk to her."

"Yeah, I bet you would," Balfour said. "Pretty hot, huh?"

Crawford laughed. "Police business, David. I think she was with Paul Mulcahy the night of his father's party. I have a few questions for her."

"Yeah," Ott said, under his breath. "Like how much does she charge?"

Crawford shook his head at him.

"Here's her number," Balfour said and gave him her cell number. "Her name is Willow, not sure what her last name is."

"Willow's good enough," Crawford said. "Thanks."

"Any time," Balfour said.

Crawford dialed the number. A woman answered.

"Hello, is this Willow?" Crawford asked.

"Yes it is, who's calling?" She said.

"My name is Detective Crawford, Palm Beach Police Department."

"O-kay," she said warily in what sounded like an eastern European accent.

"I just want to ask you a few questions," Crawford said.

"What about?"

"I'd like to meet with you in person to ask them," Crawford said.

"O-kay," she said again, even more warily.

"Can you come to the police station at 345 South County Road?" Crawford said. "Or I can come to you. Either way?"

"Okay," she said, "why don't I come there."

Crawford was guessing her accent was Polish. A little like Meryl Streep in *Sophie's Choice*.

"How is four this afternoon?" Crawford asked.

"Fine. What is the address again?"

Crawford gave it to her, thanked her, hung up and looked up at Ott.

"Just so happens," Ott said, "I'm free at four."

Crawford smiled and shook his head as his landline rang. He picked up the phone.

"Hello?"

"Charlie," it was the receptionist, "there's a guy here, a lawyer, says he represents a man named Lonnie Bates. Wants to have a word with you."

"I'll be right out," Crawford said, hanging up. Then to Ott. "A lawyer for that guy Lonnie who put the wood to us. Wants to have a word."

Ott stood. "Get ready for some serious horse-trading."

Crawford nodded and smiled. "I'm ready."

\*\*\*

## THIRTY-THREE

It looked like Crawford had been stood up. It was 4:45 and no Willow. He had just called her for a second time and he had gone straight to voicemail both times.

He dialed David Balfour. "Hey, it's Charlie," he said. "I was supposed to meet your friend, Willow, but she was a no-show. Any idea where she lives or where I can find her?"

"Sorry, man," said Balfour, "all I have is the phone number I gave you."

"Okay, well, if you talk to her, have her call me, please," Crawford said. "Explain that she really doesn't want to have a bunch of cops chasing her around."

"If she calls, I'll tell her," Balfour said.

"Thanks," Crawford said and hung up.

Then he started to call Paul Mulcahy's number, but hung up. He figured Paul had nothing to gain by helping him find Willow and, quite possibly, something to lose. If Willow was the woman with his father in the pool house, that made him a pawn at best, a pimp at worst.

So instead he went to his go-to.

"Hi, Rose," he said after she answered. "I need your help."

"Ah, let me guess, John?"

"John?"

"The cocktail party crasher."

"No, Willow, the party girl."

"Is that a cop expression?"

"One of them. The more common one, though, is *working girl*."

"Really?" Rose said. "I take umbrage at that. I'm a working girl. A very *hard* working girl."

"I know you are," Crawford said. "And the last thing I want is you taking umbrage. Any idea where I can find her?"

Rose was silent for a few moments. "I think I remember hearing that she stays at one of the hotels."

"In Palm Beach?"

"Ah-huh." Rose said. "I'd try the Colony or the Chesterfield."

"But don't they charge like four hundred a night?"

"Yeah, maybe even more," Rose said. "But I got a feeling she makes a lot more than that."

"Really?" Crawford said. "Like how much?"

Rose laughed. "I can't believe we're having a conversation about what hookers make in Palm Beach, but I bet she might pull down a thousand dollars on an *active* day."

"Or night," Crawford said. "Alright, well thanks, I'll give them a try. I appreciate it."

"You're welcome, Charlie."

Neither the Chesterfield nor the Colony had anyone named Willow staying there. Crawford was thinking of giving the Bradley Park Hotel on Sunset a call. Instead he had a thought and called back the manager of the Colony, physically identified Willow--using the photo he had--and explained that the person he was trying to contact had an accent–possibly Polish–and was staying there for the season. No one fit the bill, so he tried the Chesterfield again. This time he was in luck.

Wieslawa Nowicki was staying there for her third season in a row, the manager said, and volunteered that she was a very nice, quiet, gracious guest of the hotel. Which, to Crawford, sounded as though she was good and discreet and didn't conduct business on the premises.

Crawford got up, grabbed his jacket from the hook on the back of his office door and walked to his car.

Ten minutes later, he was at the front desk of the Chesterfield hotel, badging the receptionist. "Is Wieslawa Nowicki here?"

"Ah, no, sir, Ms. Nowicki left a little while ago," said the receptionist. "Was she expecting—"

"Yes, we had a little mix-up," Crawford said, doing his best, 'charmin'Charlie', as Rose called it. "I'll just wait here in the lobby for a while. If she doesn't come back, I'll leave her a message."

\*\*\*

He had read the *New York Times*, the *Robb Report*, looked at the pretty pictures of expensive houses in *Architectural Digest*, and had just picked up *Town & Country* when Wieslawa Nowicki walked through the front door of the Chesterfield.

He got to his feet and walked toward her. She was wearing an expensive silk skirt, a tight-fitting black blouse, and, by the time Crawford got face-to-face with her, a frown.

"I'm Charlie Crawford, Willow," he said. "We need to talk."

## THIRTY-FOUR

Crawford and Willow walked out of the Chesterfield and down Cocoanut Row.

"I am very sorry, detective," Willow said in her Polish accent. "I had an appointment that ran very late."

"Call me and tell me that next time," Crawford said sternly.

Willow nodded.

Crawford decided—what the hell, why not go all in with a big bluff. Because about three in twenty times, it worked. "Ms. Nowicki, you were seen at Knight Mulcahy's party—the night he was killed--walking down to his guest house."

Willow stopped dead in her tracks and turned toward Crawford. "Who told you this?"

"It doesn't matter," Crawford said, his eyes boring into hers. "Look, I have no reason to suspect you did anything wrong, I just need you to tell me what happened. What you saw."

She looked away and bit her lip.

"It does make me a little suspicious, though," Crawford said. "When you're a no-show at our appointment. About what you might be hiding."

She turned back to him. "I have absolutely nothing to hide," she said, then started to say something but stopped.

"What were you about to say?" Crawford asked.

She exhaled and looked away.

"It'll be so much better for you," he said, "if you just tell me the truth."

She exhaled again, but her eyes came back to him. "We had sex."

Crawford started nodding. "Okay, then afterwards?"

She exhaled again. "Then afterwards I went back up to the

party, but didn't stay long."

"And what about Mulcahy," Crawford said. "What did he do?"

"I really don't know," Willow said, "I just got dressed and left."

She looked down for a second. Then she made eye contact, but blinked a few times.

"You're not telling me everything," he said.

She nodded earnestly, but blinked some more. "Yes, I am."

"You saw someone there, didn't you?" he asked.

"No, I—"

"Yes, you did," Crawford. "Who did you see?"

She turned away.

Crawford grabbed her shoulders and turned her back so she was facing him. "Who did you see Ms. Nowicki?"

"A man," she said.

"'Where was he?" Crawford asked.

"Looking in," Willow said. "Through a window on the side."

"On the house side or the ocean side?" Crawford asked.

"The house side."

Willow tried to turn away again, but Crawford still had his hands firmly on her shoulders. "Who was he, Ms. Nowicki?"

She fixed him square in the eyes and didn't blink. "I have no idea."

"But you saw him inside at the party, right?"

"I don't know, I didn't see him very clearly through the window," she said. "I just remember he had brown hair."

"What else?" Crawford asked.

Willow shrugged. "He stepped back when I looked out, so I just saw him for a second."

"What about... do your remember what he was wearing?" Crawford asked.

"A blue jacket was all I saw."

Crawford took his hands off of her shoulders. "Was it a double-breasted blue jacket?" He motioned to his chest to indicate twin rows of buttons.

"I'm not sure, I'm really not."

***

While Crawford was interrogating Willow, Ott was on his way down to Boca Raton. He and Crawford had talked and they had agreed that Ott's objective—at this stage anyway--was just to determine whether Oglethorpe was the cocktail party crasher or not.

Ott got off of 95 and GPS'ed his way to 5 Broomsedge Lane. The house was a small brick ranch with a connected two-car garage. He parked on the street, got out, walked up to the front door and pushed the doorbell. A few moments later a man with light brown hair and a gaunt but handsome face answered the door.

"Mr. Oglethorpe?" Ott asked, flashing ID. "I'm Detective Ott."

"Yes. Can we make this fast, detective?" Oglethorpe said, walking past Ott with a garage door clicker in his left hand. "I'm on my break from work."

"Sure," Ott said, following him. "Let me just have a quick look at your car. I need to take a few photos of the front right bumper."

Oglethorpe shook his head. "Okay," he said, "but you're not gonna find anything. No bumps, no dings, no nothing. I am a very safe driver."

"I'm sure," Ott said. "Won't take more than a few minutes."

Oglethorpe pushed a button on the clicker and the garage door started to roll up.

Ott looked into the garage. There was the black BMW on one side and a small motorboat on a trailer on the other side.

Ott pulled his iPhone out of his pocket as Oglethorpe walked around to the front of the BMW.

Ott snapped off a shot, a profile of Oglethorpe's face. Then another.

Ott walked around and inspected the bumper. Then he pulled back and clicked off another three shots, all of which had Oglethorpe in them.

Then he took two steps closer to Oglethorpe and smiled. "Just like you said, no dings, no nicks, no nothing," he said. "Thank you, I appreciate your cooperation."

"No problem."

"You can go back to work now," Ott said.

Oglethorpe nodded. "Hope you catch the guy."

## THIRTY-FIVE

Leonard Burton, Lonnie Bates's lawyer, called Crawford as he was returning to the station after meeting with Wieslawa Nowicki.

"Just wanted to know what you decided, detective."

"What I decided?" Crawford said. "The ball's in your court, Mr. Burton. You been doing this long enough to know I can't guarantee your client can skate free. But it sure helps if he gives us something we can use."

"Tell you what," Burton said. "What if I bring Lonnie down to your station and you two talk it over?"

Crawford looked at his watch. "You're workin' pretty late," he said. "Yeah, sure, I'm at the station now."

"We'll be right over," Burton said, as Ott walked into Crawford's office.

"Okay," Crawford said, clicking off and looking up at Ott who was holding up his iPhone. It was a photo of William Oglethorpe.

"This is the man in the double-breasted blue blazer," Ott said. "I just went by Rose's office and she ID'ed him."

"Good job. Email it to me, so I have it," Crawford said, looking as Ott clicked the other photos of Oglethorpe. "I have a certain Wieslawa Nowicki, aka Willow, who I want to show them to."

Then Crawford filled Ott in on his conversation with her.

"So he could be our guy," Ott said, more a question than a statement.

"It would be really good to have one down, one to go," Crawford said, as his landline rang.

"Hello?"

"It's Len Burton. Me and my client are walking in right now."

"I'll be right there," Crawford said, then he clicked off and looked up at Ott. "This should be interesting. We got Lonnie Bates and his lawyer out front."

Ott smiled. "Lonnie got something he wants to get off his chest?"

"We'll see," Crawford said standing up.

\*\*\*

"Guy's name is Habib Hamdi," Lonnie Bates said. "Back when we were growing up it was Jamie Deering."

"So he converted to Islam?" Crawford asked.

Leonard Burton, Lonnie Bates, Ott, and Crawford were in the soft room, where they did interrogations. It was the step before the hard room, where they applied heavy pressure, pushing for confessions.

"Yeah," Lonnie answered Crawford's question. "Wears a robe and turban, the whole thing. One of those guys who's always telling you what a bad dude he is."

"What's he do for a job?" Ott asked.

"Steals shit," Lonnie said. "Anything he can lay his hands on. Word is he's got hisself a Ferrari. Tried to lay it off on a fence down in Miami, but it was too hot for him."

Crawford leaned in closer to Lonnie.

"I see I got your attention, detective," Lonnie said, with a smile.

"Keep goin'," Crawford said.

"Well, it's a little complicated," Lonnie said. "Word is Jamie—I still call him that—may have capped somebody who owned the Ferrari, but I'm not real clear. All's I know is he's having big trouble dumping it."

"Nobody wants to touch it?" Ott asked.

"So I hear," Lonnie said, nodding.

"Got an address for this guy?" Crawford asked.

"Think he hangs at his girlfriend's," Lonnie said. "Somewhere in Lake Worth."

"What's her name?" Ott asked, taking notes on a pad.

"Dawnesha. Dawnesha Brown," Lonnie said. "Think she does nails somewhere."

"That's all you got, Lonnie?" Crawford asked.

Leonard Burton had been pretty quiet up to that point. "Hey, man, that's plenty," he said. "Not everyday that you get a murderer handed to you."

"*If* he did it and *if* we can prove it," Crawford said. "What do you think, Mort?"

Ott chuckled. "I think my fuckin' shoulder still hurts from where Lonnie whacked me. That was more than just simple assault. What else you got, Lonnie?"

"Nothin', man."

"Where's the car?" Ott asked.

"Got no idea. Swear."

Ott glanced at Crawford. Crawford gave him an almost imperceptible nod.

"Okay, so where'd it come from then?" Ott asked.

"I don't know that neither," Lonnie said.

Ott exhaled. "Expect me to forget you tried to knock my shoulder out of its socket? Think harder."

Lonnie glanced at Leonard Burton.

"Maybe someplace in Palm Beach," Lonnie said.

"There you go again with all your *maybes*. Amir's uncle's garage?"

"Could be," said Lonnie.

Ott shook his head. "Don't gimme that—"

"Okay, okay," said Lonnie. "Definitely."

## Thirty-Six

They tracked down Dawnesha Brown at Miss Lu's Nails on Southern Boulevard in West Palm Beach late the next morning. They walked into the shop, ID'd themselves, and told her they needed to speak to her outside.

The three of them walked out of the nail salon, then Crawford and Ott turned to Dawnesha.

"Where does Habib live?" Crawford asked, under the overhang of the ramshackle strip mall.

Dawnesha's eyes skittered back and forth between the detectives.

Ott took a step closer to her. "Where Dawnesha?" he said. "We're gonna charge you with abetting a criminal, if you don't tell us right now."

Dawnesha glanced away.

"He said, 'right now,'" said Crawford. "Or your customers and co-workers are gonna see you in handcuffs."

"Not good for business," Ott added.

She looked down at the sidewalk. "411 North Pinellas Road."

"Lake Worth?" asked Crawford.

She nodded.

Ott took a step forward and got so close she could smell him. "If he calls you, don't answer," he said. "If you call him, you're goin' to jail for a long time. Understand?"

Dawnesha nodded.

"Okay, you can go back in now," Crawford said.

She turned and went back into her shop.

\*\*\*

Crawford had never gotten a search warrant this fast before.

Usually because one particular judge seemed to spend more time on the golf course than his office. But this time they caught him at the courthouse and he signed it right away after Crawford convinced him of "probable cause." That is, that they might find evidence at Habid Hamdi's house that suggested he was behind the murder of Amir Al-Jabbah.

411 North Pinellas was a bungalow with blue peeling paint and a disgruntled-looking pit bull on a chain in the front yard.

Crawford and Ott parked on the other side of the street a few houses down, got out and surveyed the scene. There were no cars in the driveway and, from what they could tell, no signs of life inside.

They walked across the street and down to 411. The pit bull eyed them and snarled.

"Want me to shoot the little bastard?" Ott asked.

"Thought you were a dog lover."

"I am," Ott said. "But that's an oversized rat."

They walked past the house and studied it from the other side.

They eyed it for a few more moments. "Not hearing a TV or anything," Crawford said. "Lights are off."

Ott nodded.

"Let's go inside, have a look," said Crawford.

They walked back to the house and Crawford opened the metal gate. The pit bull snarled louder and took a few steps toward them.

Ott glared back at it. He could be quite an effective intimidator. Crawford told him it was because of his fearsome glower, which he could turn on and off as easily as a smile. Whatever it was it seemed to work, because the bit pull just snarled like it had a stick caught in its throat and kept its distance.

They walked up to the porch and Crawford knocked on the flimsy front door.

Ott pointed down at a small, square stub of cardboard that said *Habib Hamdi* and *Bashir El-Nadal*, a yellow tack holding it up.

Crawford knocked again.

No one answered.

Crawford pushed the door with his right hand. It had plenty of give. "Bet a stiff breeze could blow it open."

"How 'bout a swift kick?" Ott asked.

"Definitely," Crawford said, and that's what he did.

The door swung in, like it was kept shut by scotch tape.

"'Come on in, boys,'" Ott said.

"'Thanks. Don't mind if I do,'" Crawford said.

The placed smelled like one half armpit and one half Mexican food.

Crawford took out his Sig Sauer 220, just in case.

Ott didn't bother.

"How could anyone live in a shithole like this?" Ott said, as they went into a combination living room and office.

Crawford pointed to a computer on a desk that had two Dos Equis empty beer cans and a red candle next to it.

"I'll check it out," Ott said, pointing at the computer and walking toward it as he pulled on a pair of latex gloves.

Crawford nodded and went toward one of the bedrooms. The bed had black sheets and was unmade. He walked over to a bureau that had change and another empty Dos Equis can on top. He saw a check, picked it up and took a look. It was from WPB Convention Center, Inc., in the amount of $844.91. It was made out to Habib Hamdi.

Crawford walked back out to the living room where Ott was sitting at the desk, clicking away on the computer.

"Looks like Hamdi works at the Convention Center in West Palm," Crawford said. "Got a check he hasn't cashed yet."

Ott swung around in the chair. "Isn't that interesting," Ott said. "Computer was on and he was on the Convention Center's website."

Crawford walked over to Ott and looked down at the computer.

"Something else," Ott said. "Take a look at who's at the convention center today and tomorrow."

Crawford glanced down at Upcoming Events and between 'Palmcom 2016-Comic Show' and 'United Association of Plumbers and Pipefitters Local Union 630,' it said, 'Law Enforcement of Southeastern US.'

"Holy shit," Crawford said, turning to Ott. "Al-Jabbah's got these guys on a mission.

"Yeah, probably a fucked up revenge plot 'cause of what happened to his daughter."

Crawford nodded. "So it's got absolutely nothin' to do with ISIS or 9/11," Crawford said. "Just a guy who hates cops."

Ott nodded. "He's got Hamdi drinkin' the Kool-Aid, too."

"Where you get that?"

"Read a bunch of his Facebook posts--" Ott pulled one up on the computer—"like...check this one out."

Crawford leaned close to read it. "Go Des Moines shooter! You got five before they got you! RIP, my brother!"

Then he remembered the five Des Moines cops shot dead several weeks before.

"Jesus, Facebook lets you get away with shit like that?" Crawford asked.

"I don't know, he got some pretty bad reactions."

"Keep reading," Crawford said, walking away. "I'm gonna check out the other bedroom."

He opened the door and was greeted by another pungent smell. Something between nail polish remover and rotten eggs. He walked over to a wide, low bureau that had various cans and plastic bottles on top. One was a drain cleaner, another for the removal of rust, a third was a pool sanitizer, which was peculiar since there was clearly no pool at 411 North Pinellas Road.

"Mort, come in here, will ya."

For a stout man, Ott moved fast. "Jesus, I think I like the piss smell better than this," he said, walking up to the bureau.

He picked up one of the cans. "Well, look-ee here," he said. "Think I used this shit to gas up model planes when I was a kid."

"And this," Crawford said, grabbing another, "got sulfuric acid in it–" pointing to the pool cleaner—"and that, for the pool they don't have."

Ott started to open a drawer, but Crawford grabbed his wrist. "Hold on, could be booby-trapped."

"Good thinking," Ott said, looking around. He knelt down and picked a long, skinny black tie off the floor and tied it around the knob on the drawer.

"Back up."

They backed away a few feet and Ott turned away and pulled the tie. Nothing happened, so he pulled the drawer open and it was filled with nails, screws and ball bearings.

Crawford turned to Ott. "Got ourselves a little bomb-making factory here."

Ott nodded. "Nitro-methane, acetone, hydrogen peroxide… yup, I'd say so." He said, then pointing. "I'm guessing these homies probably don't use that polish-remover for their nails."

Crawford put on his own pair of latex gloves and picked up a plastic bottle, inspected it, and put it down. "We better get our asses over to the Convention Center," he said taking long, quick strides out of the bedroom.

He stopped short in the living room and Ott almost plowed into him. "We got any pics of these guys?" Crawford asked.

Ott held up his iPhone. "Took one of each from Hamdi's Facebook page."

"Atta boy."

"Always thinking," Ott said as he followed Crawford out the front door.

The pit bull growled at them.

Ott just waved at him.

They walked over to the car and got in. Crawford turned to Ott. "Let me take a look at your pics of these guys," he said as Ott turned the key to the ignition.

Ott handed him his iPhone.

"I got Ron Mendoza on speed dial from the Darryl Bill murder," Crawford explained, scrolling the M's, hitting a number, then pressing speakerphone.

Mendoza was the West Palm Beach chief of police.

"Mendoza," the deep voice answered.

"Ron, this is Charlie Crawford, Palm Beach," Crawford said, "I'm here with my partner. We got a 10-24 here. Two suspects— ISIS wannabes--one works at the Convention Center, may have bombs, possibly targeting the Law Enforcement convention there."

"Ho-lee shit," Mendoza said. "All right, let me get off and make some calls. What are the names?"

"Black guy and a white guy. I'm guessing mid-twenties. Habib Hamdi is the one who works there. Bashir El-Nadal is the other one," Crawford said, spelling each for Mendoza. "Gonna email you photos."

"Thanks." Mendoza said and gave him his email address.

"We're headed there now," Crawford said.

"See you there," said Mendoza.

***

Bashir El-Nadal and Habib Hamdi were parked on the side of Okeechobee Boulevard, El-Nadal at the wheel. He was at the wheel of a fire-engine-red 1997 Peterbilt 378 semi that weighed in at 44,000 pounds and had a 475-horsepower engine. They had boosted it earlier in the day and were about to take it on its last glorious ride. Al-Jabbah's plan was masterful, El-Nadal thought. Get up a full head of steam going down Okeechobee, then pull a hard right and crash through the glass front entrance as cops from all over the south were sucking down screwdrivers and Jack

Daniels at the five o'clock welcoming cocktail party in the front main lobby.

They were expecting more than a thousand men in blue at the party, Hamdi told El-Nadal, no doubt boasting about their heroic exploits and making plans to hit the West Palm Beach titty bars after they got a good load on at taxpayers' expense.

They had met with Jabbah Al-Jabbah for the last time at Starbucks on Clematis Street in West Palm. Al-Jabbah had promised that both their families would be getting half a million dollars each, which meant El-Nadal's estranged wife and three kids and Hamdi's mother. Al-Jabbah had said over and over how they would be heroic martyrs like the men who had taken part in 9/11, only more so because their victims would be cops, who had been directly persecuting their brothers and sisters for years.

Hamdi had tried to talk him into making it a million each, which he could easily afford. But Al-Jabbah shook his head and said that he was paying them roughly one thousand dollars for everyone they would kill and that was the going rate. El-Nadal and Hamdi had looked at each other quizzically at the time, not aware that there was such a thing as a 'going rate.'

Hamdi's phone rang. He looked at the display. It was Al-Jabbah.

"Hello, my brother," Hamdi said.

"It is time," Al-Jabbah said. "Your date with destiny."

Al-Jabbah prided himself on dramatic lines like that.

"As-Salaam-Alaikum," Al-Jabbah said.

"As-Salaam-Alaikum," Hamdi said.

El-Nadal turned the key and the Peterbilt sputtered before starting up. He put his foot on the accelerator and headed for the Convention Center a mile away.

\*\*\*

First thing Ron Mendoza had done was call dispatch and put out a 10-24 alert that two suspects—maybe armed with suicide bombs—were at, or in the vicinity of, the Convention Center and everyone near there should converge on the building and be ready to shoot to kill. Then he had gotten through to the manager of the convention center and told him to evacuate the entire building immediately.

*** 

Crawford and Ott were going west on Okeechobee doing about sixty, Crawford's pistol out, when the red Peterbilt blew past them.

"Jesus Christ," Ott said, stepping on the gas. "You see that? Passenger was definitely one of our mutts."

"Well, shit," said Crawford. "Catch up."

And in ten seconds, Ott was on the Peterbilt's tail pipe, and had flipped on his lights and siren.

But instead of slowing, the Peterbilt picked up speed.

"Close the gap," Crawford said, as the Convention Center loomed up five blocks ahead.

He leaned out his window and shot at the tires of the Peterbilt. But it kept going. As Ott swung the cruiser to the left of the semi, he fired a burst into the cab.

Suddenly, the Peterbilt swerved left, cutting off their car and careening toward the front entrance of the Convention Center.

Crawford squeezed off five more shots but the Peterbilt slowed only to adjust to the sharp left turn. It bumped up a few steps and smashed through the glass front doors of the Convention Center as Ott skidded to a stop on the sidewalk in front of the building. The Peterbilt exploded on impact and the Caprice shook like it was on top of an LA earthquake as metal fragments slammed into its windshield and front body.

Crawford looked over at Ott. "You alright?"

"Yeah, but my ears are ringing like shit," Ott said, looking out through the front windshield and reaching for his door. "Doesn't look like anybody was in the lobby."

As he opened his door, Crawford noticed a nail embedded in the middle of the windshield.

Two black and white cars skidded to a stop on either side of the Caprice.

A uniform jumped out of his car and came up alongside them. "You guys all right?"

"Yeah," Crawford said, "we're fine. Guys in the truck…not doin' so well."

Cautiously, all of them walked into the lobby, their weapons drawn. Two bars were set up on either side of the lobby. There were broken bottles and glasses everywhere.

Crawford and Ott approached what was left of the Peterbilt. They looked through the driver's side window. There was no way to ID the two men inside, but there was an iPhone on the floor that, remarkably, looked intact.

Crawford picked it up and scrolled down to the most recent calls. He saw the one from just ten minutes before and looked up at Ott.

"Whaddaya know," he said. "Jabbah Al-Jabbah's number. Wishing them a bon voyage, no doubt."

"Yeah, off to the land of twenty virgins," Ott said.

Groups of cops, their weapons drawn, started coming into the lobby from outside the building where they had retreated to once Mendoza's warning had gone out. One of the cops went up to one of the bars and poured five inches of Stolichnaya into an unbroken glass. Then he took a long pull and almost drained it.

Crawford looked over at Ott.

Ott nodded as he walked toward the bar. "Don't mind if I do," he said.

## THIRTY-SEVEN

Crawford and Ott drove the battle-scarred Caprice up to Jabbah Al-Jabbah's house on Middle Road at a little before six that night. They got a lot of funny looks along the way and the shattered front windshield made for challenging visibility. They walked up to the front door and rang the doorbell.

"You b'lieve one guy lives in this place?" Ott said shaking his head and looking up at the massive 3-story front façade.

"Until a week ago, it was two," Crawford said.

A Hispanic woman in a white uniform answered the door.

"Hello," Crawford said. "We need to see, Mr. Al-Jabbah."

"I'm sorry, but he is not here," The woman said. "He is playing golf at his club."

"Thank you," Crawford said and he and Ott turned, walked down the steps and got back into their car.

"Wonder if he plays in a thobe?" Crawford said.

"What the hell's that?" Ott asked.

"Jesus, and I thought you were fashion-conscious," Crawford said. "You know, like a tunic."

Ott thought for a second. "Nah, I see him as more a madras shorts, white belt, alligator shirt kinda guy."

\*\*\*

The valet approached the Caprice at the porte-cochere of the Royal & Alien Club as if he didn't want to get anywhere near the crippled cruiser.

"We're looking for Mr. Al-Jabbah," Crawford said.

"Yes, sir. Pretty sure he just finished up," the valet said. "Probably in the men's locker room now."

"Thanks," said Crawford getting out of his car.

He and Ott walked in the front door and up to the receptionist's desk. The woman recognized them from before.

"Welcome back, gentlemen," she said, "here to see Mr. Al-Jabbah?"

"Yes," Crawford said, "down in the men's locker room."

"It's all the way at the end of the corridor," she said, "take a right there."

"Thanks," Crawford said and Ott nodded.

They walked down the corridor and Ott pushed open the door. They went into a room that had five wide sinks on the far wall with mirrors above them. Razors, cans of shaving cream, deodorant, and after-shave were placed at the back of each sink.

The first person they saw was Juke Jackson, a towel around his waist, talking to another man who was shaving in front of one of the mirrors.

Juke smiled at them and nodded.

"Hi," Crawford said. "You fellas seen Mr. Al-Jabbah?"

"Yeah, right around the corner," Juke pointed. "The main locker room."

Crawford nodded to Juke and he and Ott went around the corner into the locker room.

Jabbah Al-Jabbah, wearing beige shorts and a blue Polo shirt, was behind Elliot Segal, who was sitting on a wood bench. The two were talking.

"Mr. Al-Jabbah," Crawford shouted as he pulled out his Sig Sauer pistol.

Al-Jabbah looked across the room as Crawford and Ott approached. "You're under arrest for the murder of your nephew and the attempted—"

Al-Jabbah, in one swift motion, reached into the locker behind him, pulled out a knife from a white leather bag, grabbed Elliot Segal around the neck and yanked him up to his feet.

"I don't think so," said Al-Jabbah calmly. "Now back up and

let my friend and me walk out of here."

Crawford and Ott didn't move.

Al-Jabbah pushed the knife into Segal's neck and a thin cut opened up.

"Jesus Christ," Segal yelled, as drops of blood fell to his chest. "Do what the man says."

Crawford and Ott backed up. "Okay," Crawford said.

"And put your guns down on the floor," Al-Jabbah said.

They did as they were told.

"You will stay here and not move a muscle," Al-Jabbah said, "If I see you after I walk out, I will slit his throat and take another hostage. Do you understand?"

Crawford and Ott nodded.

"So I'm perfectly clear?"

They nodded again.

"Good," said Al-Jabbah, moving across the wide locker room, the knife tight against Segal's neck. "You follow me, you'll have his blood on your hands."

Crawford made eye contact with Elliot Segal. He had never seen so much fear in one man's eyes before.

Al-Jabbah and Segal shuffled around the corner of the locker room.

Suddenly there was a loud crack like a baseball bat hitting a home run.

"Uhhhh," came a scream of pain.

"You sonofabitch," said a voice that sounded like Juke Jackson's.

Crawford ran around the corner of the locker room and saw Al-Jabbah on the floor, his eyes shut, blood streaming from the back of his head.

Then he looked to his right and saw Juke Jackson holding a golf club.

Six or seven iron, by the look.

## THIRTY-EIGHT

At eleven the next morning, Jabbah Al-Jabbah was in the emergency room of Good Samaritan Hospital and had plenty of company: Crawford, Ott, five West Palm Beach detectives and a small army of suits from the FBI and Homeland Security. They were all there to get a crack at questioning Al-Jabbah before he was arraigned.

Crawford was talking to one of the West Palm detectives when his phone rang. It said 'Cecelia Vargas,' a name he didn't recognize but he answered anyway.

"Hello."

"Detective Crawford," said the woman's voice, whispering.

"Yes."

"It's Jacqui Mulcahy," she said. "Can you hear me?"

"Just barely," Crawford said. "Is something wrong?"

"Yes," she said quietly. "Algernon Poole forced me to write out a check for two million dollars to him this morning."

"What?" Crawford said. "When did this happen?"

"Just a few hours ago," she said. "He's a very violent man. He has kept me a hostage in my own house for the last two days. He took my cell phone, cut the house line, this is my cleaning lady's cell."

"And you had that much money in the bank?" he asked after a moment.

"After Knight's experience with Ainsley Buttrick's fund, he kept a lot of cash on hand."

"What bank?"

"Palm Beach National," Jacqui said. "Algernon made me call the manager and tell him it was okay to cash the check."

"So you think he cashed it?"

"I don't know," Jacqui said. "Knight cashed big checks like that before."

"Okay, here's what you do," Crawford said. "Go to your bedroom and lock the door. Put furniture up against it just to make sure. Me and my partner will be right there. Leave a door or two open, if you can."

"I will. Please hurry."

***

Crawford and Ott arrived at Jacqui Mulcahy's house on North Ocean ten minutes later. They went around to the back French doors, which were open and went inside. Then Crawford held up his hand and they listened for voices.

Nothing.

They went through the back porch into the living room, stopped again, and listened some more.

Still nothing.

Then they walked toward her bedroom, down a long hallway and knocked on the bedroom door.

"Who is it?" came the distraught voice of Jacqui Mulcahy.

"Crawford and Ott," Crawford said.

"Oh, thank God," Jacqui said. "Let me get the door."

It took a few moments for her to move the furniture and unlock the door.

They walked in and she looked infinitely relieved. Crawford thought for a second she was going to throw her arms around them.

"I don't know where he is," she blurted. "He took the keys to all the cars. I think I heard one of them start up two hours ago."

"Where does he live?" Crawford asked.

"The garage apartment," Jacqui said.

"We'll go check it out," Crawford said.

"Will one of you stay with me, please?" she said. "I am so

afraid of him."

"Sure," Ott said. "I will."

"And you have a gun?"

He smiled and patted above his left hip. "You're safe, I promise."

"I'll be back shortly," Crawford said, then turning back. "Do I need a key?"

She shook her head. "He always leaves it unlocked."

Crawford nodded, pretty sure how she knew that.

He walked outside to the detached four-car garage and took out his gun. There was a stairway on the left side. He walked up it, stopped to listen, and, hearing nothing, knocked on the door.

After a few moments he turned the knob, pushed the door open and walked into a living room.

Seeing nothing of interest there, he walked through it and into a large bedroom.

He went over to a frail-looking mahogany desk that had a pad on the right side. On the pad was a phone number. Then beside the number, the name 'Sidney'. Crawford put his gun back in his holster, then ripped the page off the pad and put it in the breast pocket of his jacket. He looked down at the bedspread and noticed a recessed rectangular outline on top of it, the size of a suitcase. Then he went to the large white bureau on the far side of the room and opened the top drawer. Nothing but a pair of black socks. He closed it and opened the next drawer. Nothing was in it. Same with the third and fourth drawers.

Then he went and checked out a walk-in closet. All that was there was a long wool coat, suitable more for London than Palm Beach.

He walked out of the bedroom, through the living room, down the stairs and back to the main house.

Then he went back down the long hallway and into Jacqui Mulcahy's bedroom.

"He's gone," Crawford said to Ott and Jacqui.

"How do you know?" Jacqui asked, at least partially relieved.

"There are no clothes in the bureau and closet," Crawford said. "He packed up a big, heavy suitcase on his bed--" then, turning to Ott—"I need you to check it out with me again--" then back to Jacqui—"I promise, he's not coming back."

Jacqui nodded as Ott followed Crawford to the door.

"We'll be back in a few minutes," Crawford said.

\*\*\*

They didn't find anything else in Algernon Poole's former residence.

In fact, he had left very little behind.

After five minutes of searching, Crawford reached into his pocket.

"I found this on that memo pad," Crawford said pointing. "Some guy's number."

Ott came over and looked at it. "That's a toll-free number," he said.

"It is?"

"Yeah, not just 800's; 866's are too," Ott said, pulling out his cell phone. "I'll try it."

Ott dialed the number and put it on speaker. "Welcome to World Dominion Cruise Line--"

Ott nodded a few times. "So there ya go. The guy's hopping a boat to somewhere."

Crawford nodded knowingly. "I think I know where," he said, tapping the word 'Sidney.' "Guy just can't spell for shit."

# THIRTY-NINE

Ott knocked off the 75 miles from Palm Beach to Miami in fifty-one minutes, despite the usual traffic tie-ups on 95. Crawford had been working his phone all the way down and found out that a World Dominion cruise ship was departing that afternoon for a 121-day cruise that ultimately ended up in Sydney. Crawford also spoke to the manager of Palm Beach National Bank, who confirmed that they had given a man with an English accent two million dollars in cash after Jacqui Mulcahy authorized it.

Crawford had gotten in touch with the Miami police chief and told him that he anticipated making an arrest on a ship in the Port of Miami. It was more a courtesy because he and Ott were fully authorized to arrest someone for a felony anywhere in the state, and the assault and kidnapping of Jacqui Mulcahy—even in her own home—definitely qualified as a felony. The chief asked Crawford if he needed any back-up and he told him they were good. He was pretty sure Algernon Poole wouldn't be packing an AK-47.

With a few more calls, he got permission to go aboard the boat that Poole was a passenger on. It was called the *Seven Seas* and the trip cost $78,000, which Ott pointed out was the cost of a good starter home in his neighborhood.

As Ott turned off of Biscayne Boulevard onto Port Boulevard, several massively tall cruise ships came into view.

With any luck, they were about to ruin the trip of one of their passengers.

***

Crawford and Ott took an elevator up to the highest deck of cabins. Algernon Poole's was just below the swimming pool, but far enough away from it so he wouldn't be subjected to hoot-and-hollering pool parties in the wee small hours. They got off and followed the signs to his cabin number, then knocked on the door.

No answer. Then a short Filipino in a starched uniform walked up to them with a big smile. "You gentlemen are looking for Mr. Poole?"

"Yes," Crawford said, taking his ID out of his pocket and showing it.

A frown rippled across the Filipino's face as Ott took a step forward. "You know where he is--"checking the man's name bar—"Danilo?"

"I think he may have gone to the lounge on the promenade deck," Danilo said.

"Would you please open his cabin," Crawford said.

Danilo hesitated.

"This is police business," Crawford said. "We need to make sure he's not in here."

Danilo reached in his pocket, pulled out a key and opened the door.

The cabin was a huge upgrade from Poole's garage apartment in Palm Beach. It was a duplex with lavish-looking leather furniture arranged in two seating arrangements—one focused on a 60-inch super Hi-Def Samsung TV. A stairway led up to a bedroom loft above. Off of the living room was an outdoor balcony big enough for a good-sized cocktail party, which had a big wooden, free-standing hot tub in one corner.

"Not too shabby," Ott said under his breath.

Crawford smiled. "Yeah, perfect for picking up his next rich, female victim," he said. "I'm going to check up above."

Crawford walked up the steps to the loft and noticed the large suitcase that had made the impression on Poole's bed in the garage apartment. Then he noticed a stack of new books on a desktop: *The Year of Magical Thinking* by Joan Didion, *The Five People You Meet in Heaven* by Mitch Albom and a grim-sounding title: *How We Die: Reflections of Life's Final Chapter* by Sherwin B. Nuland.

Not exactly the light-hearted page-turners he'd take on a trip.

# FORTY

They found Algernon Poole in the bar on the promenade deck at 1:15. Needless to say, he wasn't thrilled to see them.

Poole looked up, slightly glassy-eyed, rolled his eyes and gave Crawford a 'what the hell?' look of total disbelief.

Crawford didn't see the necessity to read him his rights or handcuff him. "So Mr. Poole, on your way to Sydney, I see?"

"I was," Poole said, shaking his head. "How did you find me?"

"You left behind one word and a phone number," Crawford said. "Other than that, you probably would have made a clean getaway."

Poole shook his head. "And I suppose it would be unproductive to offer you a large sum of money to let me sail off into the sunset."

"How much are you talking?" Crawford asked.

"Say… five hundred thousand dollars."

"Sorry. That'll add attempted bribery to the list of charges against you," Crawford said.

"I was just being hypothetical," Poole said.

"I'll let the judge decide that," Crawford said, patting his breast pocket. "I got a recorder here."

"You're so thorough, detective. You guys look uncomfortable standing there," Poole said, gesturing to the chairs at his table. "Why don't you—as you Yanks would say— *take a load off.*"

Crawford took a step forward, pulled out the chair and sat down. Ott followed.

Poole looked around for the waiter. "Want a drink?'

"Sure," Crawford said, then looking at Ott. "Ginger ale for you, partner; since you're drivin'."

Ott rolled his eyes.

The waiter came over and they ordered.

"Nice cabin you got there, Mr. Poole," Crawford said. "But I was curious about something."

"And what was that?" Poole asked.

"Your selection of books," Crawford said. "A little dark."

Poole looked down, wiped his mouth with a napkin, then looked back up at Crawford, not saying anything.

The waiter brought over their drinks. A Bud for Crawford, a Coke for Ott.

"There seemed to be a certain theme there," Crawford said.

"And what was that, detective?"

"Death."

Poole took a long sip of his drink, then carefully put it down, like he was working his way up to saying something momentous. But again, he said nothing.

"I was just curious," Crawford said again.

"I heard you the first time," Poole said. "You can't help yourself, can you, detective?"

"What do you mean by that?" Crawford asked.

"You have to figure out every little detail."

"Now that you mention it, I might be guilty of that."

Poole exhaled. "And you've already figured it out," he said. "About the books."

Crawford nodded. "You have something terminal, like cancer maybe?"

"Close enough," said Poole.

Crawford bowed slightly. "I'm sorry to hear that."

"Thank you," Poole said. "Does that bit of news get you thinking about being a little lenient?"

"You mean like, letting you go?"

Poole nodded and smiled.

"'Fraid not," Crawford said.

"I figured," said Poole.

"Especially since you're still a murder suspect." Crawford said.

Poole laughed. "You mean Knight Mulcahy?"

Crawford nodded.

"Not guilty," Poole said, holding up his hands. "But now I'm curious. Explain to me the motive you think I might have had to kill him."

"Money." Crawford said. "Before you launched into plan B here, you could have killed Mulcahy to marry Jacqui then live happily ever--" Crawford caught himself.

"See that's the problem. The *happily ever* part. It doesn't work, does it?" Poole said. "And just for the record, I am not a killer. Even though I tried to scare Jacqui into thinking I might once have been one."

He looked over at Ott. "Do you ever say anything?" he asked. "Or are you just the strong, silent type."

"You guys were having such a nice conversation," Ott said. "But now that you ask: you're telling us—quite convincingly—you didn't kill Mulcahy, but couldn't that just be a lie?"

"Sure," Poole, said with a little smirk. "It could be, because I have been known to tell a fib or two. But, turns out, not this time."

Crawford and Ott just studied Poole for few moments.

"Is that called the intimidating detective gaze?" Poole said. "Times two."

Crawford smiled, then looked down at their three empty glasses. "Okay, Mr. Poole, I'm afraid we're gonna have to head back up to Palm Beach now. Before the boat sets sail."

Poole sighed. "And I was so enjoying our conversation."

"Well," said Crawford. "We've got the whole car ride ahead of us."

# FORTY-ONE

Crawford and Ott were waiting for Poole to pack up his things in his cabin. "A shame this thing is going to go unused for the next 121 days," Crawford said, looking around the huge duplex.

"I know," said Ott. "I was thinking maybe I'd take my vacation two months early. Throw in a bunch of sick days I never used. Borrow some of Algernon's fashionable clothes. Always wanted to go to the Big Smoke. See that Sydney Opera House and everything."

\*\*\*

They put Algernon Poole in the cell in the basement of the station house, then drove down to William Oglethorpe's house in Boca Raton.

They got there and parked on the street. When they rang the bell there was no answer, so they went and looked through the glass part of the garage door and saw that Oglethorpe's BMW wasn't there.

They went back to the Crown Vic, got in and just waited. A half hour later they heard a car, then the garage door go up and saw, from across the street, the black BMW drive in.

They got out of their car, walked up to the front door and pushed the doorbell. A few second later Bill Oglethorpe answered the door. The expression on his face was something between surprise and annoyance.

"Hello, Mr. Oglethorpe," Ott said, "this is my partner detective Crawford. May we come in?"

Oglethorpe didn't move. "What do you want?"

"Just have a few questions," Ott said.

Oglethorpe sighed, turned, and waved them in. "You already asked me a few questions." He pointed to some chairs.

All three of them sat.

"All right, ask away," said Oglethorpe. "And let's see if we can be done with this, okay?"

"Mr. Oglethorpe, you were at the party at Knight Mulcahy's where he was killed, correct?" Crawford asked.

Oglethorpe's gaze dropped to his shoes and finally he said. "Correct."

"And the way we heard it, Knight Mulcahy told you to leave," Crawford said, "because you weren't invited, correct?"

Oglethorpe said something unintelligible.

"What?" Ott asked.

Oglethorpe eyed him with disdain. "I said, correct."

"Then, the way we heard it, Mulcahy insulted you and you threw a glass of wine in his face," Crawford said.

"It was scotch," Oglethorpe said, his toe started tapping on the sisal rug. "Shitty scotch."

"And then Mulcahy forcefully escorted you to the front door and, apparently threw you down some steps," Crawford said.

"Let's just say, two steps," Oglethorpe said.

"Close enough," Ott said.

"Then you went to your car--"

Oglethorpe shook his head, violently almost. "What the hell's the point of all this?"

"Mulcahy was killed not long after he pushed you down the steps," Crawford said softly.

"And we're after his killer," Ott said.

Oglethorpe looked back and forth between them. "And you think it might be me?"

"Convince us otherwise," Crawford said.

Oglethorpe was silent for a few moments. "This is the most absurd thing I've ever heard," he said.

"We get that a lot," Ott said. "Like my partner said, *convince us.*"

"So I got in my car and left," Oglethorpe said.

"Not the way we heard it," said Crawford. "We heard you got in your car, then a few seconds later opened the door, got out and walked around the house."

"Like maybe you had some unfinished business to take care of," Ott said.

"Yeah, the unfinished business was taking a piss."

"And you had to walk around the whole house to do that?" Ott asked.

Oglethorpe glared at Ott, then Crawford. "You got the wrong guy," he said. "Keep looking."

"I'll say it again...*convince us*," Ott said. "And what's the deal anyway, goin' around crashing parties, what's that all about?"

For a second, Oglethorpe looked both embarrassed and chastened. Then: "Is that a crime?"

"No, but it's kinda weird," Ott said.

All of a sudden, all of the air seemed to slowly seep out of Bill Oglethorpe and a very sad look appeared on his face. Then he gave a little half smile and turned almost sheepish. "I try to be an...addition. I try to bring something to the party, I guess you would say. People don't seem to mind. I'm a pleasant enough guy. I have good manners and social graces--" Ott shot a quick glance at Crawford, like, *where is he going with this?*—"plus what Jacqui said."

"Wait, what?" Crawford said.

"Mulcahy's wife, Jacqui," Oglethorpe said.

"Yeah, what about her?" Ott said.

"I was talking to her at another party about a month ago, she said I'd be welcome at any party she ever gave."

"So are you saying," Crawford said, "that you were actually invited to their party?"

Oglethorpe eyes went into a thousand-yard stare. "No," he said softly.

"So you *weren't* invited to the Mulcahy party?" Ott asked.

Oglethorpe shook his head and looked forlorn. "Guess she forgot," he said.

"So going back to what we were talking about," Crawford said. "You got out of your car, took a leak, then what?"

Oglethorpe was still locked in the thousand-yard stare. "I just went around and looked in the window…at her. At Jacqui. She's such a beautiful woman. Why in God's name she ever married that…Neanderthal…."

***

It was 4:30. Crawford and Ott were headed back up to Palm Beach.

"I've said it before and I'll say it again," Ott said.

"What's that, Mort?"

"Only in Palm Beach," Ott said. "Just a lonely, delusional guy who wouldn't hurt a flea."

Crawford nodded as Ott pulled onto 95. "Yeah, and for us, one more dead-end street."

## FORTY-TWO

Crawford and Ott were in Crawford's office looking at the whiteboard a half hour later. It was 5:30 and it had been a long day. Crawford had just put lines through Algernon Poole and MWDBBB. Aside from the fact that Oglethorpe was clearly not the type to shoot somebody, even if he'd just been thrown out of someone's house, the time-line, they realized, was off: Algernon Poole had seen Oglethorpe get into his BMW--the second time--at least forty five minutes before Knight had been killed.

Still on the list of Knight Mulcahy suspects were Chuffer Church, Ainsley Buttrick, Ned Durrell, Sam Pratt, and Earl Hardin.

"Gotta tell ya, Charlie," Ott said, slouched down on the chair facing Crawford. "Same old, same old. Nobody's jumpin' out at me."

"Yeah, I know," Crawford said. "All we got is—compliments of my friend Willow—*maybe* brown hair and *maybe* a blue jacket. So that means everyone except Ainsley Buttrick is in the mix."

"Yeah, but I wouldn't rule him out," Ott said.

Crawford shook his head. "I'm not," he said. "And when you think about it, we also got close to a hundred other guys at the party. Could be any one of them too. Someone else might have a motive we don't even know about."

"Yeah," Ott said. "You think we gotta start all over again?"

Crawford sighed. "I don't know. Let's go down the list one last time."

Ott nodded and yawned at the same time.

"Okay. I just don't see Church, Pratt, and Durrell," Crawford said. "I mean, none of 'em could stand Mulcahy, but I don't see that as being enough to kill him. Just not enough there."

"So you're goin' with Buttrick or Hardin?" Ott asked.

Crawford nodded. "Yeah, but not with a lot of conviction.

Buttrick just struck me as a guy who could get really nasty, even though he played it down. Said Mulcahy trashing him on the air was like a gnat on the ass of an elephant."

"He said that?" Ott asked with a smile.

"No, that's my interpretation."

"And Hardin going out the French doors looking like he was a man on a mission," Crawford said. "Problem is we don't know what time that was."

"Yeah," Ott said, "not only that but I got the sense he's on your short list 'cause of how you feel about him."

Crawford thought for a second, then nodded. "Yeah, you might be onto something. Which ain't exactly professional."

They fell silent for a minute or two, suspects and motives churning around in their heads. Finally, Crawford, who had been looking out his window at the full moon, turned to Ott. "Remember when we met with Skagg Magwood, how he said Earl Hardin and Sam Pratt were in the line-up for Mulcahy's show the week after he bought it?"

Ott nodded. "Sort of."

"That's what he said," Crawford said. "I wonder if there's anything there?"

"You mean like Mulcahy was about to drop a bomb or something?"

Crawford nodded. "You never know," he said. "I mean, maybe he found out about Hardin's cozy little arrangement with that real-estate flipper. Rose Clarke couldn't be the only one who knew about it. I'm guessing Mulcahy had a bunch of sources."

"So maybe he was about to go public with it," Ott said.

"Yeah, imagine if you were about to get outed for having a three-million-dollar a year scam…wouldn't you want to shut up the Mouth of the South?"

"Damn right," Ott said.

"We gotta talk to him again," Crawford said. "I'll call him first thing tomorrow morning."

"And Sam Pratt?" Ott said. "Wonder what Mulcahy was going to say about him? Magwood mentioned a play, didn't he?"

"Yeah," said Crawford. "No details, though. Didn't sound like much at the time."

"But what was your sense about the guy, Pratt?" Ott asked. "You spent five hours with him on the golf course."

"Yeah," Crawford said. "Then another hour and a half in the men's locker room afterwards."

"And?"

"Like I told you, good guy, I liked him."

"He wouldn't be the first likable guy to ever kill someone," Ott said.

Crawford nodded. "Yeah, I guess maybe I really want it to be Hardin, a guy who really is *not* a good guy."

Ott started to say something, but Crawford held up his hands. "I know," Crawford cut him off. "Unprofessional again, so shoot me."

Crawford looked at his watch and got to his feet.

"Where you headed now?" Ott asked.

"Got a dinner."

"Oh, yeah, with who?"

"Rose," Crawford said wearily. "It's like a payback for intel she came up with. You know, shit you shoulda come up with."

"Fuck off," Ott said, shaking his head. "You forgetting all that stuff I got on the Al-Jabbah?"

"Yeah, okay, I take it back," Crawford said, yawning.

"I swear," Ott said, shaking his head. "Like going out to dinner with Rose is heavy lifting. Any time you want me to sub for you, just gimme the word."

Crawford grabbed his jacket, then turned to Ott. "Thanks for the generous offer, Mort, I would have, but—"

"But what?"

"I thought tonight was your bowling night."

## FORTY-THREE

Rose was dressed to the nines: Maximum cleavage, minimum skirt length. Way, way more skin—taut, lean skin—than clothing material.

Crawford was wearing blue jeans, a blue sport shirt, and a cream-colored white jacket, his treat to himself: a 40% off mark-down from Jos. A. Bank.

As a pair, they were what Crawford's mother would have referred to as a "cute couple."

They had talked a lot about Rose's recent real-estate deals. Her latest two being a $50 million house on the ocean bought by one of the latest internet billionaires, who had graduated from high school just six years before, and the other for a mere $17 million, sold to a professional golfer from Australia.

"So I'm buying," Rose said. "And we're getting a bottle of the best champagne in the house."

"No, Rose, that wasn't our deal," Crawford said. "I'm buying and we're getting a perfectly good bottle of Moet & Chandon."

"That'll do," Rose said. "Why'd you pick that?"

"Had it at my wedding," Crawford said. "Way too much of it."

Rose smiled. "Whatever became of Mrs. Charlie Crawford?"

"Miranda? She married a very successful orthopedic surgeon in New York," Crawford said. "House in Southampton, ski place in Telluride, Colorado. Couldn't put ol' Charlie the cop in the rear-view mirror fast enough."

"I bet that's not true," Rose said.

"Trust me," Crawford said, seeing his segue opportunity. "Speaking of New York, I got a question for you: you know anything about Sam Pratt and a play he might have been involved in. Maybe having to do with Knight Mulcahy."

"Scammin' Sammy, you mean," Rose said. "And you bet it had

to do with Knight Mulcahy. That whole thing really took the cake, though not a lot of people know about it."

Crawford raised his hands. "Well, come on, tell me all about it."

"Let's order first," Rose said.

Crawford ordered the steak and Rose the veal chops and the waiter poured two flutes of Moet.

"So what happened was, Sam—who always teeters on the edge of financial destitution, maybe because he's hardly ever worked in his life--came up with this scheme--"

"Also, known as a scam?"

Rose was nodding prodigiously. "Absolutely. So he went to a few people, who I think he felt had more money than brains. One of whom was—"

"Knight Mulcahy."

"Exactly," Rose said. "So he conned Knight into thinking he had gone to college with a producer who was going to do a remake of that play *Six Degrees of Separation*--"

"Oldie but a goodie."

Rose nodded. "So Sam got Knight interested because he was smart enough to play to Knight's massive ego and told him he wanted him to be Executive Producer. Then he did something else really smart."

Crawford signaled for Rose to go on.

"You know that actor Trent Payne? Canadian guy, I think," Rose asked. "Guy who was in *Drayton Hall*, that TV series back in the 90s with a big cult following?"

"Kind of," Crawford said.

"Well, apparently ol' Trent hadn't had a role, except maybe dinner theater, in like fifteen or twenty years and was about as strapped for cash as Sam. So Sam gets Knight to put up twenty-five grand for what he called a "commitment fee" and gives Trent half of it to come have lunch with Knight and sell him on how he and Julia Roberts are going to be in it. And how it's gonna be the biggest thing since *Hamilton*."

Crawford had leaned in so far that his face was a foot away from Rose's. "And Mulcahy bought it?"

"Hook, line, and sinker."

"That's incredible. How long ago was this?"

"Only about three months ago."

"So how'd it turn out?"

Rose took a long pull on her second glass of champagne. "This stuff's not half bad," she said. "So Sam gets Knight to put up another 250k to be Executive Producer, sends him the script, and tells him about all these Broadway actors who are gonna be in it. Then a month goes by, then another...then...crickets."

Crawford flagged the waiter down again. He poured out the rest of the bottle.

"One more bottle?" Rose asked.

"I gotta be at the office early tomorrow," Crawford protested.

"So," said Rose, "some days you just gotta play hurt."

She smiled at the waiter and asked him to get another bottle.

"So keep goin'," Crawford said.

"Okay, so then Sam goes into no call-back mode," Rose said. "Knight's callin' him like twenty times a day and Sam's not answering. Finally Knight goes to his house and confronts him. And, the way I heard it, Sam finally confesses."

"Wait, that he scammed him?"

Rose laughed. "No, way more creative than that. That his old college buddy, the producer, absconded with the money and went to Switzerland. And Sam's looking high and low but can't find him anywhere."

"Sounds like Sam shoulda been in the play," Crawford said. "Guy seems like a hell of an actor."

"I know, right?" Rose said. "So then Knight puts a PI on the case who—fifty grand later—gets to the bottom of it."

"How long ago was that?"

"Not long," Rose said. "Maybe two weeks."

And there it was, Crawford realized: Knight Mulcahy was about to go public with the whole story. Spin it, probably, to make it seem he wasn't such a dupe as he apparently had been, but in any case, make Sam Pratt out to be the sleaziest con artist who had ever walked the mean streets of Palm Beach. Not to mention probably have him prosecuted for swindling, defrauding, grifting, and whatever else he could come up with.

Pratt's days in Palm Beach would be numbered and his next residence would likely be a jail cell somewhere in a bad neighborhood of Florida.

Or maybe up in North Carolina, bunking in a cell next to fellow scam man Bernie Madoff.

## FORTY-FOUR

It was eight the next morning and Crawford was playing hurt. He wasn't sure he did his best work the morning after imbibing at least a bottle of champagne all by himself, but he wasn't about to tell Ott about it. He did fill him in about Sam Pratt's phantom play, though, and Ott hung on his every word, much as Crawford had the night before. Ott shook his head a number of times and chuckled appreciatively at Pratt's con-man creativity.

Earlier, Crawford had called both Pratt and Earl Hardin and left messages for them to call him. He wasn't going to hold his breath but unless he heard back from them by eleven or so, he and Ott were going to go to Pratt's house and Hardin's office.

"I woke up in the middle of the night thinking about Hardin," Ott said. "Here's the problem I see: To cover his ass, he could just say he came up with a price for those little old ladies' houses that needed work and the ladies were good with his prices. Then he had a buyer who specialized in fixing up old, beater houses. Happens every day, right?"

Crawford shrugged. "Yeah, I guess. It's probably no crime, but you sure as hell can make a case he was playing fast and loose with the ethics."

"How do you figure that?"

"Well, so you make a shitload of money off of one little old lady… okay, maybe that doesn't raise eyebrows. You do it five or six times over the course of a couple of years, that does. It's pretty damn clear to me—and Rose Clarke—that he was taking advantage of their trust. And if the world suddenly finds out—"

"Okay, but Pratt's still my leading contender," Ott said.

"Mine, too," Crawford said as his phone rang.

Crawford didn't recognize the number, but clicked the green circle. "Hello."

"Detective Crawford," said a woman's voice. "This is Laurie

Pratt. I got your message on our landline and just wanted to tell you my husband is out of the country."

Crawford turned to Ott and mouthed, 'Pratt's wife.' "Thanks for the call, Mrs. Pratt. And when will he be getting back?"

"I'm not exactly sure," she said. "He's in Switzerland on business. He might be there for a while."

"Could you give me his cell phone number?" Crawford asked.

"Ah, sure," she said, reeling it off. "But he told me he doesn't have very good service there. Kind of spotty."

"Okay," Crawford said. "When he did leave?"

"Yesterday morning," she said.

"Flew out of Miami, I assume?" Crawford asked.

"Yes, ah-huh," she said.

"Well, thank you very much," Crawford said. "When he calls, will you ask him to call me right away."

"Yes, absolutely," she said. "I will. Goodbye, detective."

Crawford hung up and looked out his window for a few seconds. Then, back at Ott. "I'm not buying a word of that."

"What did she say?"

"First of all, that Pratt is in Switzerland on business."

"Went there to see his fictitious producer friend about his fictitious play, no doubt?"

Crawford nodded. "Yeah, something in her tone I just didn't buy."

"So, simple enough," Ott said. "I check all flights from Miami to Geneva and Zurich. Where else?"

"Umm, Basel maybe?"

Ott chuckled. "Aced that gut in geography, huh?"

\*\*\*

Crawford was right. No Sam or Samuel Pratt on any flights from Miami to any airport in Switzerland, though Ott had someone double-checking to be absolutely sure.

And, as predicted, no call from Earl Hardin by eleven o'clock. Crawford and Ott decided to go to Hardin's Bush Island office and drop in. Afterward they planned to swing by Sam Pratt's Golfview Road house unannounced. In the meantime, Crawford sent two detectives to keep an eye on Pratt's house—to see whether he came or went.

***

The receptionist at Earl Hardin's office asked for Crawford and Ott's names when they walked in and asked for Hardin, then went back to get him. A minute later she came back out and said he wasn't there, must have gone out the back door.

Crawford glanced at Ott and Ott shook his head. "You mean, when you told him our names?"

"Oh, no, sir," the receptionist protested. "He wasn't there. Probably had a showing."

"Do you have a picture of Mr. Hardin?" Crawford asked.

The receptionist nodded and said, "Yes, sir, in this brochure." She handed him a brochure. Earl Hardin had a big unctuous smile and a flaming red bow tie.

Crawford and Ott thanked her and left.

Back in the car, Ott turned to Crawford. "What now?"

Crawford shrugged. "What can we do? Can't drive around Bush Island all day trying to find the guy."

"Go to Sam Pratt's house?"

Crawford nodded.

"Gonna be kind of embarrassing," Ott said. "Interviewing someone I saw naked."

***

It took them forty minutes to get to Pratt's house. Laurie Pratt answered the door, shading her eyes with her hand. "Yes?"

"I'm detective Crawford, spoke to you earlier," he said. "This is detective Ott."

"Oh, yes," she said, not inviting them in.

"Mrs. Pratt," Crawford said. "We need to speak to your husband."

"But, I told you--"

Ott cut her off. "I checked all flights from Miami to Switzerland yesterday and your husband wasn't on any of them."

Laurie cocked her head, going for a shocked look. "Well...well, maybe he flew to Italy and drove up."

"I tried Milan too," Ott said.

"Mrs. Pratt," Crawford asked, "are you aware of your husband's efforts to finance and produce a Broadway play?"

Her face flushed and she glanced away. "I don't know much about it. Just that in the end it didn't work out."

Crawford nodded. "We believe that your husband might still be here somewhere. Maybe he said he was going to Switzerland but changed his mind," he said, giving her an out.

"What we want to avoid, Mrs. Pratt, is ratcheting up our hunt for you husband," Ott said. "We don't want to make it a public thing, where the whole town knows we're pursuing him. So when you speak to him, please have him check in with us."

She started nodding. "Oh, I will, I will. I'll definitely try to reach him—" she looked at her watch—"it's five o'clock over there now. I'll try to catch him before dinner."

"Thank you, " Crawford said. "Oh, do you have a photo of your husband?"

She looked at him suspiciously. "What do you want it for?"

"We just like to keep a record of everyone we interrogate," Crawford said.

"But you haven't interrogated him yet."

"No, but we will, sooner or later," Crawford said.

She looked like she had bought it. "Okay, wait a sec."

A minute later she came back with a picture of her husband.

"Thank you, Mrs. Pratt," Crawford said.

Ott nodded and they walked down the steps to their car.

"He's here," Ott said as he turned the ignition key.

"Yeah, I know," Crawford said.

"What's with the photos?" Ott asked.

"I'm going to pay a visit to my friend Willow," Crawford said. "See if she can ID either of them."

"Good thinkin'," Ott said.

"Time to head back up to Bush Island," Crawford said.

"What if Hardin ducks us again?" Ott asked.

"I got a tried and true method to make sure he doesn't," Crawford said. "We have to make a quick pit stop at the station first."

\*\*\*

They went down to Dominica McCarthy's cubicle in CSEU and explained that they needed her help.

After they spent a few minutes on the website for Earl Hardin's real-estate company, Dominica dialed her phone.

"Yes, hello," she said, "my name is Abigail Carnegie and I would like to go see one of the houses I saw on your website."

"Oh, yes, Mrs. Carnegie, which one?" the receptionist asked solicitously.

"414 South Beach Road," Dominica said.

"If you'll hold for a second, I'll get the agent whose listing that is," said the receptionist.

"Yes, but explain to him that I need to see it right away, my plane leaves from Stuart--"the local private airport—"to St. Barth's at 2 o'clock this afternoon."

"I'll tell him," said the receptionist.

The smarmy voice of Earl Hardin came on right away. "Hello,

Mrs. Carnegie, this is Earl Hardin," he said. "We can see the house at 414 South Beach Road right away. The owners are up north now."

"Very good, let's make it 12:30," Dominica said.

"Excellent," said Hardin. "Are you the New York Carnegies or the Pittsburgh ones?"

Dominica was not prepared to answer any question about her made-up heritage. "Does it matter?"

"No, I just—"

"See you at 12:30," Dominica said and hung up.

Crawford greeted her with a high five.

"More like the South-Miami-Beach-by-way-of-Brooklyn Carnegies," she said.

## FORTY-FIVE

Crawford and Ott were waiting in the driveway as Hardin drove up to 414 South Beach Road in his Mercedes S550. His disgust became apparent as he got parallel to their Crown Vic, the replacement for their wounded warrior Caprice.

Crawford rolled down his window. "Sorry, Mrs. Carnegie got a flat and asked us to come in her place."

Hardin was steaming. "I've had just about enough of you assholes," he said, shaking his head.

"Likewise," Ott muttered.

"At least you didn't have to come down to Palm Beach this time," Crawford said. "We needed to talk to you and clearly you've been unresponsive to our calls. So your car or ours?"

Hardin glanced over at the grimy Crown Vic and shook his head in disgust. "I wouldn't get in that piece of shit if you paid me."

Crawford laughed as he and Ott got out of their car and walked over to the Mercedes. Crawford opened the passenger side door as Ott got in back.

"Pretty nice," Crawford said, inspecting the instrument panel. "But how's it on gas?"

"Some of us don't have to worry about shit like that," Hardin said.

"Thanks to the Elizabeth Raymonds, Harriet Norbeths, and Martha Brinkerhoffs of the world, right?" Crawford had gotten from Rose the names of some of the little old ladies whose houses Hardin had sold in the last two years.

"What's the question?" Hardin asked with a mile-wide frown.

Bluffing time again. "We heard something about how Knight Mulcahy was going to expose you—well, maybe that's too strong—was going to *suggest* that maybe you didn't have the best interests of certain clients of yours in mind when selling their houses. Word is, maybe you went straight to a certain buyer and made deals before your clients houses were even on the market. I'm hearing the local real-estate board might frown on such a practice."

"Yeah, and if all the details came out," Ott said, "it might hurt your business *and* your lily-white reputation. People like Abigail Carnegie might not want to deal with you."

Crawford continued the one-two punch. "And maybe the best way to prevent all that from happening," he said, "was to silence the Mouth of the South."

"That would be Knight Mulcahy," Ott said.

Hardin shook his head in disgust and glared at Ott, then Crawford for a full five seconds.

"So are you *really* suggesting I killed Knight Mulcahy?"

"Question is, are you denying you killed Knight Mulcahy?" Crawford asked.

"I am denying it loud and fucking clear," Hardin said. "And I want you clowns to stop harassing me or you're going to have a nice, fat lawsuit."

"All we're hearing is that your alibi is you left the party early—went out the back door, not far from the pool house where Mulcahy got killed—got home and watched something on the Golf Channel," Crawford said. "No witnesses, nothing to back up your story."

Hardin turned away from Crawford and thumped his steering wheel lightly for a few moments. Finally, he turned back to Crawford and lowered his voice. "Call up Jenny Bayliss and you'll get all the alibi you need."

"Who is Jenny Bayliss?" Crawford asked.

Crawford sighed. "A new agent in our office. She lives in Bush Inlet Colony, just south of Bush Island."

Crawford snuck a smile at Ott.

"So you went there after Mulcahy's party?" Crawford asked.

Hardin nodded without making eye contact.

Crawford glanced back at Ott and smiled. "To watch the Golf Channel, I'm guessing."

*\*\**

Sure enough, Hardin was at Jenny Bayliss's house from eight forty five to ten o'clock. Bayliss said she knew that for a fact because she took off her watch right before the two of them climbed into her hot tub, and her watch read 8:50. That was at least forty five minutes before Paul Mulcahy saw his father walk out the back of the house with Olivia Griswold and an hour and fifteen minutes before the ME estimated Mulcahy's time of death.

After they met with Bayliss, they went by the Chesterfield Hotel after Crawford contacted Wieslawa Nowicki on her cell. She met them in the lobby and looked at the two pictures of Hardin and Pratt. Then she shook her head and said she was sorry but she couldn't ID either one. She just didn't get a good enough look, she said. But then she added that if she had to choose, it would be Pratt.

Sam Pratt was still on the lam. Crawford had called his wife, who said she still hadn't heard a word from him. She mentioned the poor cell service again and Crawford said, 'ah-huh' again. Ott had been on his computer for more than an hour, trying to see if he could find anything more about Pratt's theater scam. Crawford was in his office, when Ott came storming in.

"Bein' kind of a movie guy," Ott started excitedly, "you're gonna love this."

"Whatcha got?"

"Okay, remember, back twenty years ago when that Canadian actress got killed on a set up in Vancouver?"

Crawford didn't hesitate "Yeah, sure, Danielle DeRham," he said. "I had the big-time hots for her when I was a teenager."

"Well, they never found out who did it," Ott said. "Primary suspect was this actor by the name of Torben Belz."

Crawford put his feet up on his desk and cocked his head.

"Where you goin' with this?"

"I remember tellin' you how I thought Sam Pratt might be Canadian," Ott said. "Him saying 'a-boat' instead of 'about'"–Crawford leaned closer to Ott–"So I found out Pratt was, in fact, born in Toronto. And, get this, he moved down here and married this woman who was one of the producers of that movie Danielle DeRham was killed in."

Crawford slid his feet off the desk and sat up straight. "Holy shit, are you kidding me?"

Ott smiled wide and nodded. "Nope," he said. "Just thought you'd want to know."

"Damn right I do," Crawford said. "But I got a million questions."

"Fire away."

"Okay," Crawford said. "So, first of all, how did all this come onto your radar in the first place?"

"You know I always start with Google–"

Crawford nodded.

"So I Googled Pratt, having no idea what I'd come up with, and the first thing I found out was he changed his name legally twenty years ago from Torben Belz to Samuel Billingsley Pratt."

Crawford started tapping his desk. "But to become a citizen they do a background check, fingerprints, the whole deal, right?"

"Yeah, but marrying an American citizen makes it a hell of a lot easier," Ott said. "Still, there're a bunch of hoops you gotta jump through. Like you said, a background check for one–where they want to know your previous address and place and date of birth. Plus there's fingerprints, petitioning the court, the whole nine."

"And what about arrest records?"

"That, too."

"Well, so if he was the leading suspect in Danielle DeRham—"

"He was never arrested and never charged," Ott said. "So nothing ever showed up. You can be a suspect all day long and be asked a million questions, but you know how it is, nothing's in the public record if you're never charged."

Crawford nodded. "So keep going, he marries the woman producer, then what?"

"Okay, so I was on the phone a good part of the morning. Tracked down the lead detective on DeRham at Vancouver PD. He's retired now. He remembered just about everything, though. Told me word was ol' Torben was banging both the producer and Danielle at the same time. Seems like he started straying when he got a whiff of Danielle on the set."

"What's the producer's name?" Crawford asked.

"Nancy Pulitzer," Ott said.

"Okay, so the obvious quest—"

"What was Torben/Sam's motive to kill Danielle?"

"Yeah?"

"According to the lead again, Torben had this really nasty, public fight with Danielle over something," Ott said. "Supposedly the director had to get between 'em before they scratched each other's eyes out."

"About what?" Crawford said. "What was the fight about?"

"Well, bear in mind, this was twenty years ago," Ott said. "But seems like Danielle was pissed off Torben was two timing her. And apparently he was trying to shut her up so word didn't get back to his meal ticket, Nancy."

"Okay so he married Nancy to get his green card, presumably," Crawford said. "But he's married to Laurie now. What happened to Nancy?"

"Well, so she married him, but it had a real short run. Like Sam's movie career," Ott said. "Only lasted two years. Then Sam tried to revive it, but there wasn't much to revive. So a few years later—about ten years back—he marries Laurie. For love apparently, because she's as poor as a church mouse."

"Which is why he had to run the scam on Mulcahy," said Crawford.

"Exactly," said Ott as Crawford's cell rang.

\*\*\*

Two plainclothes cops, Stan Gilhuley and Jon Evans, were across the street from Sam Pratt's house on Golfview. Gilhuley, in the driver's seat, had nodded off a few minutes earlier and Evans was playing poker on his iPhone, when there was a tap on his window. Evans looked up and saw a man with a gun pointed at him.

"Hands up, boys," said Sam Pratt.

Gilhuley woke up and both he and Evans put their hands up as Sam Pratt opened the back driver side door and slid in.

"So what are you doing here?" Pratt asked. "As if I didn't know."

Gilhuley shot a glance at Evans, then said: "We're just—"

"Looking to put your handcuffs on me?" Pratt said.

Gilhuley and Evans were mum.

"Well, instead of that, we're gonna do it the other way around," Pratt said. "You, Mr. Driver, take your handcuffs out and put them around the wrists of Mr. Passenger."

Nobody moved.

"Hurry the hell up," Pratt said, gesturing with his gun.

Evans put his hands out as Gilhuley reached for his cuffs.

"Whoa-whoa-wait," Pratt said to Gilhuley. "Where's your gun?"

"Shoulder holster," Gilhuley said, motioning with his head.

Pratt leaned forward, reached inside Gilhuley's jacket with his left hand while putting his gun up to Gilhuley's head. He found Gilhuley's pistol and slid it out of the shoulder holster. Evans kept his hands out in front of him.

"Okay, now Mr. Driver, take your cuffs out and put them on Mr. Passenger's wrists."

Gilhuley did as he was told.

"They look pretty loose," Pratt said. "Tighten 'em up. Don't want Mr. Passenger sliding out of those things, trying to be a hero."

Gilhuley tightened up the handcuffs on Evan's wrists.

"Much better," said Pratt. "Now, Mr. Passenger, do the same thing to Mr. Driver."

Evans reached down, got his handcuffs, opened them and put them around Gilhuley's outstretched wrists.

"Come on, a little tighter," said Pratt.

Evans tightened them.

"Very good," said Pratt. "Now don't you boys feel totally helpless?"

Neither answered the question.

"So tell me what you're doing here," Pratt said.

Gilhuley shifted uneasily but neither one spoke.

Pratt put the gun up to Gilhuley's head. "Tell me," he said.

"We're just s'posed to see whether you came back to your house," Gilhuley said.

"Well, looks like you fucked up," Pratt said. "Like I snuck in without you spotting me."

Gilhuley nodded. "Yeah, I guess so."

"So then what?" Pratt said. "Let me guess, you were gonna call my buddy, Charlie Crawford. Tell him I was back."

Neither Gilhuley nor Evans answered.

Pratt pressed the gun against Gilhuley's head.

"Yeah," Gilhuley said. "That was the plan."

"Well, just so you boys don't feel bad," Pratt said. "I been here all along. No Switzerland, no nothing, not yet anyway. I'm thinking of going to someplace that doesn't have reciprocity with the US."

Pratt pulled the gun back from Gilhuley's head.

"I'm gonna make a quick phone call," Pratt said, putting the gun down on the seat.

Pratt held his iPhone with one hand and dialed with the other.

As he did, Gilhuley slowly moved his left hand up to the door handle, where Pratt couldn't see.

Then, suddenly he yanked the handle up, and bolted out of the driver's seat. He had taken eight strides before Pratt picked up his Beretta Px4 Storm, aimed it and squeezed the trigger. On his tenth stride, Gilhuley went down, catching a bullet in the back of the thigh and another in the shoulder.

"Stupid bastard," said Sam Pratt, jumping out of the back seat, then going through the open door into the driver's seat.

He aimed the pistol at Evans. "Don't be as dumb as your partner."

Evans put up his hands. "Please," he said. "I'm not gonna do anything."

Pratt turned the ignition key. The Caprice started up and Pratt floored it.

***

Crawford looked down at the display on his iPhone. It said, 'Gilhuley.' He clicked it.

"Yeah, Gil, what's goin' on?"

"I got hit," Gilhuley said, "Sam Pratt. He just took off with Evans as his hostage."

"Oh, Jesus," Crawford said. "You gonna be okay? Where are you?"

"Lawn across from Pratt's house on Golfview–"

Crawford yelled at Ott. "Get an ambulance over to 19 Golfview, house across from it. First responders, whoever else, get 'em there fast."

Ott nodded and started dialing.

"You gonna be all right, Stan?" Crawford asked again.

"Yeah, just losin' a little blood here," Gilhuley said. "I'll be okay. You gotta get Pratt before he does something to Evans."

"We will." Crawford said. "So he took off? Any idea where

he's heading?""""

"South. Then outta the country, he said."

"Okay. You got something you can use as a tourniquet?" Crawford asked, getting up and grabbing his jacket from behind his office door.

"Nah, I'm cuffed. Wait, I hear a siren," Gilhuley said.

"They'll be there before you know it," Crawford said, signaling to Ott to follow him. "We're gonna go get Evans now."

# FORTY-SIX

"Where we goin'?" Evans asked Sam Pratt as they went down South Ocean.

Pratt was doing the speed limit, not wanting to attract any more attention than a police car normally attracts.

"Cuba," said Pratt.

"You serious?"

"Think I'd tell you?" Pratt said. "If your partner hadn't gone and fucked things up, you two would be in a closet in my house and me and my wife would have been headed to the airport."

As Pratt went past Mar-a-lago, he saw a police car up ahead pulled over to the other side of the road with its light bar going, but no siren.

Pratt slowed down, then took a left into a driveway.

It was the entrance to the Beach and Racquet Club, known as the B & R.

Pratt looked into his rear-view mirror and saw that the police car had followed them in.

"Shit," Pratt said, rolling up to the front entrance of the club.

Two young guys wearing khakis and polo shirts with the club insignia on their breast pockets were standing next to the front door. One of them came up to Pratt.

"Can we park your car, sir?" he said. "What's your membership num—"

Pratt raised the Beretta and smiled. "I'm a member of the gun club, not the B & R."

The kid's eyes got huge and he backed away.

The driver of the police car was keeping his distance. He was on the phone with someone.

Pratt looked over at Evans and pointed his gun. "Let's go," he said. "We're goin' inside. Shove over."

Evans slid over close to the door as Pratt slipped over next to him. "You're gonna get out slowly and I'm gonna be right behind you. Then I'm gonna put my hand around your neck and you're gonna be cool. No panic, no blood. Got it?"

Evans nodded.

***

"It's definitely the car," the cop in the car at the B & R parking lot said to Crawford. "He's just sitting there next to Evans. Wait— they're getting out now."

Crawford was speeding south on South Ocean, just north of Mar-a-lago.

"They got out on the passenger side. Guy's got a gun to Evans' head," the cop said. "They're backing up into the main entrance of the club."

"Okay," said Crawford. "Stay where you are. Don't move, don't get out of your car, don't do a damn thing."

"Copy that," said the cop.

"Me and Ott are almost there—" then, turning to Ott—"we got a hostage negotiator?"

Ott thought for a second. "Bostwick did one once," he said, "but he's on vacation."

"Guess we got the job," Crawford said. "Hope like hell we got a bull horn in the trunk."

***

"Nice and easy," Pratt said to Evans as they backed into the club. "Atta boy."

Pratt turned his head and saw a large woman dressed in a beige skirt and a blue blazer that had a Beach and Racquet insignia on the breast pocket.

"Sir, what is the meaning of this?" she said, apparently not intimidated by the 9 millimeter pistol in Pratt's right hand.

Pratt eyed her. "We're gonna be using the facilities for a while," he said. "Hope that's okay with you."

The woman cocked her head to one side. "I remember you," she said. "Weren't you guests of the Goodwins one night for dinner?"

"Yeah," Pratt said, backing down a long wide corridor. "Now cut the chit-chat and go tell the cops I'm gonna blow this guy's head off if they do anything stupid."

The woman didn't move.

Pratt gestured menacingly with his gun. "Go on, do it."

The woman walked toward the front door of the B & R and went out.

Crawford, Ott, and about twenty plainclothes and uniformed cops were huddled up outside of the B & R. There were eleven marked and unmarked cars parked haphazardly in the parking lot. Light bars were flashing, no sirens. Crawford was addressing them when the woman walked out of the main entrance waving her hands frantically.

"That man's got a gun," she said. "I'm terribly worried about our members and staff."

Crawford walked over to her. "Did he say anything to you?"

"Yes, that he was going to shoot the man with him if you did anything stupid."

"Where is he?" Crawford asked.

"At the end of the corridor," the woman said. "I think he went into a room that we use for meetings."

"Where are the other exit and egress points in the club?" Crawford asked.

The woman told them of four other ways to get inside and about how there were two pools on the ocean side along with various changing rooms, and on the other side, six tennis courts.

After she described the lay-out of the club, Crawford thanked her, huddled up with the men again, and laid out a plan. Basically, it was for the others to block all ways of escape, but not to get anywhere near Pratt and Evans.

Crawford and Ott were going to go in the front entrance and try to engage Pratt in conversation.

Additionally, Crawford had put in a call to Jack Ingleby, a sharpshooter who had just driven up. Ingleby was decked out in a chest-protector and helmet and had a L129A1 gas-operated sniper rifle with an elaborate scope slung over his shoulder.

Crawford and Ott walked over to him as he got out of his car.

'Thanks for getting here so fast," Crawford said. "Subject's in a room at the end of a long corridor. We're going in there—" he pointed to the front entrance—"try to talk to him. Maybe you can get a shot from outside."

"Through one of those sidelights maybe," Ott said, pointing at the narrow windows on either side of the front door.

"Okay," said Ingleby, "I'll check it out. I just want to make sure he can't spot me."

"Yeah, definitely," said Crawford, then he and Ott nodded and walked toward the other cops. A few moments later they all fanned out to the sides and the back of the club, while Crawford, bullhorn in hand, and Ott walked in the front entrance.

Right away, Crawford saw Pratt and Evans at the end of the long corridor. Pratt was sitting on a long, wide mahogany conference table facing them, while Evans, in hand cuffs, stood in front of him. The room had a door in the middle with sidelights on either side.

Crawford put the bullhorn up to his mouth. "We're both unarmed, Mr. Pratt. We took off our jackets, so you can see. We're here to make this end—" his first thought was to say, 'without bloodshed'– but he said instead, "without incident."

"Well, good," Pratt shouted. "Come a little closer so you don't have to use that thing and I don't have to shout."

Crawford and Ott walked down the corridor until they were about fifteen feet from the door to the meeting room and stopped.

"How's this?" Crawford asked.

"That's good. Nice to see you again, Charlie," Pratt said.

Crawford nodded. "Yeah, wish it was under different circumstances."

"So I've had a little time to think," Pratt said, "and I'm not real keen on having one of those long stalemates you see in movies—"

"Okay, so how you want to play it?"

"Very simple," Pratt said. "I want a helicopter to land on one of the tennis courts, so he can take me where I tell him to go."

Crawford thought for a second.

"This isn't something you need to think about, Charlie—" There it was again— 'a-boat' instead of 'about.' "It's how it's goin' down and it's non-negotiable. Also, I want a million dollars in the front seat of that chopper. Travel expenses, let's call it. So get on your phone and make it happen. You're a 'can do' kinda guy, right?"

Crawford had already alerted Norm Rutledge to what the situation was and told him to be expecting a call. "I'm going to reach into my pocket now," Crawford said, "get my cell, and call the chief of police, okay?"

"Yes, go ahead," Pratt said.

Crawford pulled out his iPhone and dialed. Rutledge picked up on the first ring.

"Yeah?"

"I'm here at the Beach & Racquet Club with Mr. Pratt and his hostage, Jon Evans. Mr. Pratt has asked for a helicopter with a million dollars in it to land on one of the tennis courts here."

"What the fuck, Charlie," Rutledge said. "I can't do that."

Crawford had hoped for a better answer from Rutledge, but wasn't really surprised.

"I know you can't do it immediately," Crawford said. "But will you make the necessary calls."

"Like to who?" Rutledge said. "I can't just pull a helicopter and a million bucks outta my ass."

Crawford smiled. "Great," he said. "So why don't I call you back in, say, fifteen minutes and see where things stand—"

"Five minutes," Pratt said.

Crawford nodded. "Okay, five minutes." Then like he was listening to Rutledge. "Yeah, I agree, talk to the mayor and check Palm Beach County Park Airport, see what helicopters they got available. Yeah, perfect, sounds good."

Crawford clicked off with Rutledge and looked up at Pratt. "We're on it."

Pratt was nodding. "I see that," he said. "There are dozens of choppers around here. And coming up with a million bucks, that's kids' stuff."

"Yeah, but you have to give us a little time," Crawford said.

All of a sudden Ott cleared his throat and spoke. "How 'bout you substitute me for Officer Evans, Mr. Pratt?"

Pratt studied him suspiciously. "Why, what's the difference?" he said, then with a smile. "Except maybe you're a little easier to hide behind."

Ott smiled back. "Yeah, well, there's that," he said. "Not to mention, Officer Evans has a wife and kids. I don't."

Pratt shook his head. "Nah, we'd have to go through the whole handcuff thing. Takin' em off and putting 'em on."

"I'll just have my partner put 'em on me," Ott said. "Then walk over to you and switch places with Officer Evans."

"And in that split second, give your sniper out there a shot at me?" Said Pratt. "I want you, Pudge—" he pointed to Ott— "to go get his rifle and bring it back to me."

Ott nodded, walked toward the front door, opened it and went outside.

A moment later he walked back in holding the sniper's rifle in both arms in front of him.

When Ott was twenty feet away, Pratt pointed to the floor. "Okay, put it down on the floor and slide it over here."

Ott did.

"Good man," Pratt said, picking it up and putting it to one side of him.

Crawford and Ott just stared at Pratt for a few uncomfortable moments. Finally, Crawford thought, what the hell, why not ask?

"Why did you kill Knight Mulcahy, Mr. Pratt?" he asked.

"What's this Mr. Pratt stuff?" Pratt said with a smile. "Out there on the golf course it was Sam and Charlie, newfound friends."

"Okay then, why'd you kill Knight Mulcahy, *Sam?*"

"'Cause the fat shit couldn't keep his mouth shut."

"That's it," Crawford said. "That's a reason to kill a guy?"

"Ask around, Charlie," Pratt said. "Half the town wanted to kill the bastard. You probably know that by now."

Crawford's cell phone rang. It was Rutledge. "Yeah, Norm?"

"We're not on speaker, right?"

"No."

"Okay, here's the long and the short," Rutledge said. "I can get a chopper there, but no way in hell a million bucks. Even spoke to national Patrolman's Benevolent; nobody can authorize it in a hurry."

"Okay, that's good, Norm," Crawford said. "How long 'til it gets here?"

"About a half hour," Rutledge said, "but you heard me about the money, right?"

"Yeah, sure did, that's great."

Pratt waved his hand. "Put him on speaker," he said.

"Sure," Crawford said, clicking the speakerphone button.

"Putting you on speaker, Norm."

"Okay," said Rutledge.

"Repeat what you just said about the helicopter, Norm," Crawford said.

"It's gonna get there in about a half hour," Rutledge said.

"Make damn sure it's got a full tank," Pratt said. "I don't want to get in it and find out we can only go ten miles."

"Don't worry," Rutledge said, "we're not playing games with you."

"Better not," Pratt said. "Or else Officer Evans wife and kids will be deep in mourning."

Crawford nodded. "Okay, thanks, Norm," he said, clicking off.

Crawford caught Pratt's eye. "So where you thinking about going, Sam?"

"Disneyworld," Pratt said.

Crawford laughed. "No, really."

"I don't know," Pratt said. "A full tank—three hundred miles or so—that can get me to a lot of nice places. Havana, Nassau, I've always wanted to go to Harbor Island."

Crawford nodded as a plan came into his head. "Look, Sam, I'll be honest with you, we're having a hard time getting the money," he said. "But I think I got the answer."

"Damn well better," Pratt said, agitated.

"Just listen," Crawford said. "Remember when Pedro Bacalao's son was kidnapped last year?"

"Yeah, they cut off his ear to show they weren't screwin' around," Pratt said. "What about it?"

"My partner and I caught the guys who did it," Crawford said. "Mr. Bacalao was very grateful. He pledged a generous contribution to the Palm Beach Police Foundation."

"Yeah, what did I read?" Pratt said. "Couple million?"

"Three million, to be exact," Crawford said. "So I'm thinking maybe we could get him to release a million of that."

"I like the way you're thinkin'. Give the man a call," Pratt said. "What could be a better cause than saving a cop's life. Right, Jon?"

Evans, pistol to his head, didn't give him the satisfaction of reacting.

"This'll take a little more than a phone call," Crawford said. "I gotta talk to the guy in person."

"Why?"

"Why?" Crawford said. "'Cause I can't just call him up and say, *I need a million bucks.*"

Pratt thought for a second, then stood up behind Jon Evans.

"All right, Charlie, but I want Pudge –" he pointed his pistol at Ott—"to go. And for the sake of Jon here, he better be very persuasive with Bacalao." Pratt said, then to Ott. "Take my number and keep me up to speed on what's happening. Charlie, you stick around."

## FORTY-SEVEN

Turned out Pedro Bacalao, the heir to the largest pharmacy chain in South America, was in Bogota on business. Not only that, no one was authorized to release any of the money from the Palm Beach Police Foundation's account until the full board met and approved it. None of this was going to keep Ott from going forward with the plan.

He dialed Sam Pratt a half hour after leaving the B&R on his cell phone. "Yeah, Pudge, what's up?" Pratt said.

"I got a million dollars," said Ott.

"I love a can-do guy," said Pratt.

"I'm coming back to the B & R now. I'll meet you at the helicopter that'll be landing in about ten minutes," said Ott.

"You're the best," Pratt said. "I'll raise a glass to you in Harbor Island or Havana or Nassau, wherever I end up."

"Just live up to your part of the bargain and release Evans," Ott said.

"Don't worry, he'll be back on a stake-out before you know it."

\*\*\*

Pratt, pistol to Evan's head, was walking through the B & R on his way out to the tennis courts. He got to a pair of French doors and looked out. There on the center court was a bright blue Bell Jet Ranger helicopter, its blade going half speed.

"I see the chopper," Pratt said into his cell, "where are you?"

No response.

"Where the hell are you?" Pratt said, as he pushed open the French doors.

Positioned on the roof above the French doors, Ott jumped. As he landed on Pratt's shoulders, he knocked the pistol out of his hand.

Within seconds, twenty cops with their guns drawn were surrounding them, including Crawford who had run out through the French doors.

Ott, his favorite brown polyester pants ripped at the knee, straddled a prostrate Pratt and looked up at Crawford.

"Hell of a jump, Pudge," Crawford said.

Ott slowly shook his head and smiled. "I'm *way* too old for this shit, Charlie."

## FORTY-EIGHT

Ott had reinjured an old football injury in his right knee when he landed.

Rose Clarke, who had gotten wind of what happened at the B&R, had called Crawford who had filled her in. He told her about Ott's leaping heroics and his bum knee. Then she thanked him, hung up and called Ott.

"Mort, how you feeling?" she asked.

"Fine, Rose," Ott said. "Just hobbling around with this damn cane for a while."

"Well, I'm just glad you didn't break anything," she said. "How 'bout I take you out for dinner? Pick you up at your place at seven tonight. I've got this great out-of-the-way spot. Really good food."

*What the hell*, Ott thought. *Beat the hell out of the Marie Callender chicken pot-pie in the on-deck circle in his freezer.*

He gave her his address, then, with a big grin on his face, walked into Crawford's office.

Crawford, on his computer, looked up. "Hey, Mort, you feelin' any better?"

Ott nodded. "Like a million bucks."

"So that Advil kicked in?"

"Nope," said Ott, shaking his head. "'Cause I got a dinner date with the hottest chick in the whole state of Florida."

"Don't tell me," Crawford said. "Some babe from your bowling league?"

"Funny. How 'bout Rose Clarke?"

A frown cut across Crawford's face. "Really?"

"I knew she'd eventually see the light. Realize you were just another pretty face."

\*\*\*

Turned out to be a bit of a hike from Palm Beach, but Rose promised Ott it would be worth the drive.

They parked, walked in and sat down in a corner in the back.

Rose pointed to his leg. "You want to rest it on a chair?" she asked. "Would that be more comfortable?"

"No, I'm fine, thanks," he said. "It really is no big deal."

"Are you just being stoical?" Rose asked.

"Nah. Hey, I like sympathy as much as the next guy," Ott said, taking a drink of water. "It just doesn't feel all that bad."

"You really jumped off the roof of the B&R?"

Ott nodded sheepishly. "Seemed like a good idea at the time."

"That's like out of some cowboy movie or something," she said, beaming.

"Yeah, well, best I could come up with on short notice," he said

Rose put her hand on Ott's. "My hero."

He laughed as he heard footsteps off to one side.

"Welcome, to Marbella," the waiter said, instantly recognizing Ott, but not missing a beat. "Hello, detective...and madame... tonight we have two incredible specials. May I tell you about them?"

Ott smiled up at him. "Sure, Bill. Whatcha got?"


### THE END


I hope you liked *Deadly*. If so, please go to Amazon and give it a review.

A native New Englander, Tom dropped out of college and ran a Vermont bar—straight into the ground. After limping back to college to get his diploma, Tom became an advertising copywriter, first in Boston then New York. After ten years of post-Mad Men life, he made a radical change and got a job in Manhattan commercial real estate. Not long after that he ended up in Palm Beach, buying, renovating and selling houses while collecting a lot of raw material for his novels. On the side, he wrote Palm Beach Nasty and a screenplay called Dead in the Water. While at a wedding a few years back, he fell for the charm of Charleston, South Carolina. He moved there and wrote Palm Beach Poison and a series set in Charleston. Recently, wandering Tom moved again. This time, just down the road to Skidaway Island, outside of Savannah, where he just completed Palm Beach Deadly.

69132159R00157

Manufactured by Amazon.com
Columbia, SC
06 April 2017